LINDA

Also by Anne Alexander

THE PINK DRESS

LINDA

Anne Alexander

DOUBLEDAY & COMPANY, INC.

GARDEN CITY, NEW YORK

Library of Congress Catalog Card Number 64–16235
Copyright © 1964 by Anne Alexander
All Rights Reserved
Printed in the United States of America

DEDICATED
to
BARBARA, CAROL, *and* SHARON,
three daughters grand,
and to
DEBBIE, KAREN, *and* KATHY,
three granddaughters.

LINDA

CHAPTER I

THE BIG QUESTION

Today was the last day. She either asked or she didn't; it was as simple as that. Linda dressed quickly and carefully. She needed to look her best because of Doug. If only her insides would stop doing flip flops! *We'll meet accidentally after English, as we always do,* she planned, *and I'll say very casually, "About the Fall Frolic . . ."* She smiled at her reflection in the mirror the way she'd smile at Doug.

Linda heard her three brothers clatter down the stairs. They'd give her a bad time if they knew her intent—especially Tim, who probably assumed she'd already asked George. Tim, two years younger than she, and a mere freshman at Claremar High, had been asked the day the Fall Frolic was officially announced.

As Linda selected a bow for her hair that would match the blue of her dress she heard a knock on her door. "Yes?"

"Better hurry, princess!" her father called. "It's getting late."

"Be right down, Dad." Linda shoved her night clothes into the closet and hastily smoothed over the bedspread. Tomorrow she'd straighten her room and make her bed properly for sure.

She took a final look in the mirror. Her blue dress was one of those "just-right" dresses for occasions like today when she needed extra confidence and courage. Girl-ask-boy affairs were always awkward, she decided—especially when the boy was someone *special*, like Doug. If only there was still a tomorrow in which to ask! But there wasn't. Linda took a deep breath. She felt shaky just thinking about asking.

The family hadn't waited for her; they were already eating. Linda slid into her seat at the table. "Sorry," she apologized. Johnny and Jeff, her twin brothers, sat across from her. They always looked like scrubbed angels on Cub Scout day, only they never were. She saw them study her.

"Look, Mom," Johnny said, "Linda's wearing a Sunday dress."

"Why's she dressed up?" asked Jeff.

Linda sipped her juice, hoping that Mom was to busy to comment.

"You look great," said Dad. "Blue's your color, princess."

Linda almost sighed her relief. Dad approved. That meant Mom would too. Maybe this was the first time she'd worn the blue to school, but it hadn't been bought for just a Sunday dress.

"Something doing?" Mom asked. She placed a platter of French toast and bacon on the table.

"Must be," said Tim. "Something for her paper, I bet." He speared a couple of slices of French toast from the platter and coated them with strawberry jam. "Right, sis?"

"More likely the exchange scholarship," said Dad. "An interview, perhaps?"

Linda felt her cheeks burn. The American Field Service, the school newspaper—both so important to her. But somehow the Fall Frolic and Doug were important too. Only she couldn't see herself explaining. "I—I just wanted to wear this," she said lamely. "That's all."

"You know what?" Johnny waved his fork importantly at Mom. "This guy in our class says when girls dress special they're chasing boys."

"Yeah," added Jeff, "and you better watch out, 'cause maybe you're the one." He eyed Linda critically, then sniffed. "You even smell pretty," he concluded.

Linda knew that she was the color of a beet. She turned helplessly toward Dad.

"All right, boys, stop it," he commanded. "I approve, no matter what the reason. You look—enchanting, princess." His eyes twinkled. "Now how's for some food? Pass me your plate." He held out his hand.

Linda shook her head. She knew that anything she ate would remain a solid, unyielding lump. She felt so nervous, she was even having difficulty swallowing her juice. "Just this," she said, motioning to her glass. "I guess I'm not hungry."

"I'll take her share, Dad." Tim reached across the table and speared two more slices.

"Tim, your manners!" Mom looked as if she'd like to rap him across his knuckles. She turned to Linda. "You're not coming down with something, are you?"

"I'm just not hungry."

"Anyone need a ride this morning?" Dad asked. "I'll be driving that way on the way to the depot." He commuted the short distance to San Francisco on the train.

Linda shook her head. Beth was driving this morning. Tim wouldn't be needing a ride, either. He loped to school each morning with a buddy—"to develop leg muscles," he claimed. One needed all sorts of muscles for football.

"We'll ride," said Jeff.

"Speaking of rides, sis, how's about me and Angela hitching one with you and George to the dance?" Tim glanced quickly at Linda, then riveted his gaze to his plate. "I mean—well, I can't drive a car yet, and, well, I mean you're my sister and all, but you're still better than parents." Tim's voice changed pitch as he spoke, and Linda could see the tips of his ears redden.

"I—I haven't asked anyone yet," she said.

"What?" Tim's head shot up and he looked squarely at Linda. "Today's the last day. Why? I mean, Angela asked me right away. How come you—"

"I know," Linda interrupted. "Didn't you think she was —sort of too eager, maybe?"

"Heck, no." Tim laughed. "I knew she was asking me even before she did. Her girl friend phoned to clue me in. But George—how come you're letting him sweat it out?"

"That's why the fancy dress," said Johnny. "She's chasing George."

Tim shook his head. "She doesn't dress to impress George."

"Then who's she chasing?" asked Jeff.

"You *are* asking George, aren't you?" Tim demanded. "I mean, after all . . ."

"Excuse me." Linda pushed back her chair. "I'll get the lunches. Beth said she might be by early." She felt shaky, anxious to get away from the inquisitive eyes of her family. She took out the four lunch bags and left the three larger ones on the drainboard. "'By, everybody," she said.

"Wait a minute," Tim commanded. "About George."

"I haven't time." Linda kissed her parents quickly and bolted for the door. In her room she gathered together her books, took a last look at herself, and dabbed on a little more perfume. Maybe now she'd smell even prettier. *Please let me ask him right,* she pleaded silently. She heard the family in hot debate as she opened the front door.

"Wait, Linda."

Linda turned as her mother walked across the room to the hall. If only she wouldn't nag about George!

"I just wanted to say good luck, darling." Mom's smile was a warm caress. "With whomever you ask," she added.

Linda kissed her mother on the cheek. "Thanks, Mom." She grinned ruefully. "I'll need it."

While she waited for Beth, Linda tried to sort out her thoughts. She felt guilty about George. Everyone expected her to ask him. He was a convenient date, and about as exciting as yesterday's cold mashed potatoes. They were good friends, with a friendship cemented by a mutual love of journalism, and nothing more. Their dating during their two high-school years was a sort of joint agreement suggested by their parents, who were friends, and continued through laziness. She hoped that George didn't assume she was asking him. He had mentioned the dance a couple of times but she'd changed the subject. Actually George was probably as ready as she to terminate their dull dates.

Beth barely stopped the car long enough for Linda to get in. "Guess what," she greeted. "Mom said I could have a dinner." Beth's blue-green eyes danced with excitement. "For the eight of us. Let's start planning."

"When? Why? What eight?"

"Before the dance, silly—the Fall Frolic. You and George, me and Steve—I can't figure whether it would be better to have ham or turkey or something real special, like squab with wild rice—"

"I've never had squab," Linda interrupted. "Let's have something everybody knows about."

"Me neither," Beth admitted. "But it sounded so, oh, sort of different and dramatic, and maybe— Okay, turkey or ham." Beth pulled in to the student parking lot. "So what else shall we have? Mashed potatoes, sweet potatoes— No"—she interrupted herself—"let's not plan now. Let's go find Mary Lou and Vickie and tell them."

A regular whirlwind, Dad called Beth. Linda quickened her step to keep pace. No wonder Beth was head cheerleader. She was energetic, enthusiastic, and, Linda thought, positively beautiful.

"Look," Beth said, digging into her purse. "I almost forgot." She pulled out a swatch of material. "My dress."

As Beth turned to her Linda felt as though her friend were actually seeing her for the first time that day. Beth's eyes widened in surprise. "Hey!" she exclaimed. "What's the occasion? You're wearing your blue. Something special?"

Linda held the swatch Beth handed her. Now was the moment to confide. "Sort of," she said. "I thought maybe—"

"There's Mary Lou. Let's tell her," Beth interrupted.

About Doug? Linda felt momentary shock, and then she realized that Beth wasn't listening. She was with her future dinner party. "You tell her," Linda said. "I'll go on to English. Okay?"

"See you."

Linda watched Beth dash off. She was like quicksilver:

mercurial—and fun. Her excitement was contagious. Linda could feel her own enthusiasm and confidence build up. What a perfect thing—to be able to mention the dinner party along with the dance. Doug was in luck. The dinner would be swank, with everything just so, the way Beth's home always was—everything in its right place, and never confused and messy, the way a home with three brothers gets. Beth didn't even have a sister.

As she opened her locker to store her lunch and excess books, Linda noticed that she still held Beth's swatch. She put it in her purse and started up the hall to class. Between English and French she'd see Doug. She could hardly wait.

"What's the rush, princess?" Linda looked up, startled. Doug! He fell in step with her. "Pretty dress."

"Thank you." The sheer pleasure of just walking with him almost engulfed her, and she hoped she wasn't grinning like an idiot. "Why'd you call me that?" she asked.

"Princess? It just popped out. Maybe because you look like one today. Maybe because I think blue's a royal color. You figure it out."

"Dad calls me princess," Linda explained. "Mom's the queen, he says. Because of my brothers." Linda knew she wasn't making much sense. She felt as though her brain were all thumbs . . .

"Here we are." Doug stopped in front of her English room. "See you after class. Okay, princess?"

Now Doug sounded teasing. Linda watched him go—tall, broad-shouldered, close-cropped brown hair that might curl if it were longer. His brown eyes with their flecks of gold had looked glad to see her. And he planned to see her again after class. Everything was working out beautifully. Just fifty minutes from now she'd ask.

By period's end Linda hadn't taken down many notes on Poe, but she'd rehearsed in her mind her words to Doug over and over again. She let half the class file out before she picked up her books. She didn't want to look too eager.

Doug was waiting at the door. "Hi again," he said. His smile lit his face, making crinkles around his eyes. No one, not even Tim, had a smile as cute as Doug.

Linda drew a shaky breath. This was it. "Doug," she said, "I've something to ask you."

"Ask away, princess."

Linda put her hand on his arm. "About the Fall Frolic," she said, and she gave him the warm smile she'd practiced.

There was a sudden blankness to his eyes, a stiffness to his face.

"Would you—are you—I mean, will you go with me?" She felt almost relief that now the words were finally said, although she knew her cheeks were fiery red.

He swallowed. His eyes looked stony, almost angry. "No," he said bluntly. "Sorry." He turned on his heel and left, abruptly, quickly.

Linda stood rooted, looking after him. Students milled about, going into their classrooms, but still she stood. He'd turned her down *cold*, without a word of explanation, as though she'd humiliated him by asking. Humiliated *him*? How many had heard his refusal? Linda set her teeth against her embarrassment. Her legs felt wooden as she walked alone down the hall. A bell rang and Linda knew she was late for French. Now she would have to get a tardy slip.

In the office Linda listened as the attendance secretary concluded a telephone conversation. She was checking out an absence. It didn't pay to cut at Claremar, Linda noted dully. You always got caught.

The secretary read Linda's admittance slip before she initialed it. "No reason?" she asked.

Linda shook her head. You couldn't very well put down that a boy had been inexcusably rude, could you? She turned to leave the office.

"Linda?" She turned back at the secretary's voice. "That's such a lovely dress, dear."

"Thank you." Linda's voice almost broke. A lovely dress, fit for a princess, a royal dress. Just the thing to wear for a royal brush-off.

CHAPTER 2

GEORGIE PORGIE

By noon Linda felt that she'd lived with her embarrassment so long that it was a part of her. Walking into each classroom was an effort. Maybe Doug hadn't shouted his refusal there in the hall, but he hadn't whispered it, either. Casual preclass banter took on hidden meanings. *Who had overheard?*

By noon Linda also had reached a conclusion. She would conform and do what was expected. She would take George to the Fall Frolic. Having exchanged lunch bag for books, she slammed her locker shut and slowly walked out of the school building. She would join the others on the lawn under "their" tree for lunch as they'd done every nice day since they were freshmen. What was the difference, she wondered, between conformity and being in a rut?

"Hurry!" called Mary Lou. "I'm practicing manners. And I'm starved."

Vickie, the fourth of the "inseparables," as Mom called them, looked up with a smile. "For Beth's dinner," she explained. "There's even a correct way to pass salt."

Linda grinned as she sat down. "Mom's tried to teach that to the twins," she said. She took out a sandwich and unwrapped it.

"Wow, how come the dress, Linda?" Mary Lou's words

were blurred as she talked over a mouthful of sandwich.

"It's because Linda's going to—" began Beth, and then she stopped and looked at Linda. "I didn't even listen when you started to tell me," she admitted.

Linda busied herself unwrapping her cookies. "Why a reason?" she asked, making her voice casual. "Here, have some."

"Always wear blue." Mary Lou helped herself to a couple of cookies. "It does things for you." She turned to Beth. "The dinner," she said. "It sounds absolutely perf!"

"My dress," said Beth, rooting through her purse. "Think Steve will—"

"Here. I have it." Linda handed the swatch to Beth, who passed it on to Vickie and Mary Lou.

"Natch," said Mary Lou. "Imagine being at a dinner party with *the* Steve Atkins!"

"Claremar's finest," added Vickie.

Linda watched Beth beam. Steve Atkins, young hopeful of the varsity football team, was Claremar High's best catch. Beth had done herself proud. Claremar High took its football seriously, and the town of Claremar was one of the hottest football towns in the state.

"Saw you talking to that Doug Johnson." Mary Lou arched her eyebrows at Linda. "Cute," she continued. "Too bad you couldn't ask him instead of George."

"Doug's a nobody," Vickie said sharply.

"New, isn't he?" asked Beth.

"A transfer last spring," Vickie said scornfully. "With that build he should be out for football."

"Don't get so steamed up." Beth chuckled. "You sound like a scout for Coach Wallace." She stood up and brushed the crumbs from her dress. "Besides, Linda always asks George."

"Have you told him about the dinner?" asked Mary Lou. "I haven't seen my date yet."

Linda swallowed. "No," she said slowly. "As a matter of fact, I haven't even asked him to the dance yet. I'm going to in journalism."

"What? Honestly, Linda." Beth shook her head. "Poor George, sweating it out."

"You did buy your ticket, though," Vickie said. "Didn't you?"

As Linda shook her head, Beth reached out her hand and pulled her friend to her feet. "Get it now, right now," Beth commanded. "They go off sale at three."

"Okay." Linda started off obediently, glad to get away.

"Don't forget," Beth called, "I've got cheering practice after school. Wait in the car if you want a ride."

Linda looked up and down the main corridor. Somewhere there should be a ticket salesgirl. She'd been stumbling over them for a couple of weeks. She saw Angela, Tim's date, scooting down the hallway. The girl gave Linda a shy smile.

"Hi, Angela," Linda greeted her. "You look busy."

"I'm not really." Angela smiled apologetically. "I'm trying to sell tickets, only everyone has them."

"Lucky us." Linda opened her purse. "I need one."

As Angela wrote down the names, Linda caught a glimpse of Doug striding down the hall. She wanted to hurry Angela. She wanted to hide.

"You're my only junior." Angela handed Linda the tickets. "I know you and George will have fun." Her voice sounded loud, and Linda knew that Doug had heard.

"We will," she answered. "We always do." Her own voice sounded shrill, and she knew that it must carry to Doug, as she wanted it to. At least he'd realize he wasn't the only boy in the world.

Her two afternoon classes, biology and journalism, were at opposite ends of the school. The lab experiment had taken just a little longer than it should. Now she had to rush or incur a second tardy for the day. Linda hurried as fast as she could without running. She was brought to an abrupt halt by Vickie.

"About the dance—" Vickie began breathlessly.

"I'll be late," Linda protested.

"Listen," Vickie insisted, "I was talking to the ticket chairman. She says—"

"Vickie, I bought the ticket. I'll be late." Linda brushed past Vickie. "Call me," she added.

Just under the wire. Linda slipped into her seat as the bell rang. George was already at work at his desk. He looked up, smiled, and bent over his work again. George was a *comfortable* date, at any rate. He'd like the dinner party too. She'd tell him about it in a couple of minutes. Right now there was work to do. Her galley proofs needed reading.

Journalism was Linda's favorite class and subject. She loved working on the *Clarion*. Right now she read with sharpened pencil in hand, scanning for transposed letters, a missing comma. This year she was second-page editor. Next year, she hoped, she would be editor-in-chief.

George was the sports-page editor. She heard him conferring with Mr. Hall, their instructor and advisor, and glanced up to see the two of them bend over George's page layouts. There was a camaraderie about this class that was so strong it seemed almost touchable. It was a sort of friendly communication between teacher and student and between the students. Linda picked up a fresh strip of galley. Her editorial. If there were anything she would want to change on the *Clarion,* it would be the *tone* of the editorials. They were never caustic or issue-taking like those in regular papers, but bland and mild, because that's what Mr. Hall and Mr. Marsh, the principal, wanted. So that's what she wrote. This week's "School Spirit and Football Games," for instance, was hardly necessary, when the stands were always packed for every game and the townspeople vied with students for seats.

Linda glanced over again at George. Now was the time. He was alone, leaning back in his seat, his hands clasped behind his head, a satisfied smile on his face.

Linda walked over. "Finished?" she asked.

George waved his hand across the layout. "Everything fitted like a dream," he said.

"It looks great," Linda said. "Alive." She paused. Somehow even telling old George about the dinner and asking him to the dance was giving her butterflies. She took a deep breath. "About the Fall Frolic—" she began.

"Your page finished?" George interrupted.

Linda looked at him, puzzled. "Just about, I guess," she said. "But about the Fall Frolic, Beth's giving a dinner first. We're invited." She smiled warmly down at him.

"You're asking me to the dance?"

"Yes. Of course. And Beth's dinner party."

"A little late, aren't you?" George's voice was hard. "Like today's the last day."

"I know."

"And I'm going with someone else."

"Somebody else asked you?" Linda was incredulous.

"Surprised, aren't you? Imagine anyone else's asking poor old George." His voice was heavy with sarcasm. "Well, someone did—about the time I mentioned the dance to you, only you played dense. I figured at first maybe I was obligated to you. Only—" He clasped his hands behind his head again and looked at her. "What happened?" he asked. "Did you chicken, or were you turned down?"

Linda turned away abruptly. She didn't trust herself to answer. Somehow she was back in her seat and hunched over her proofs. Frantically, she blinked back her tears. If this period would only end!

"Linda."

Linda glanced sideways, recognized Mr. Hall's tweed jacket, and forced herself to look up.

"Would you—" He broke off. "What's wrong?" he asked. "Anything I can do?"

"Nothing. It's nothing." Linda tried to ward off the kindness in his voice.

"Would you like to be excused? A drink of water, maybe?"

Walk out of the room? She couldn't. "I'm okay, really."

"See me after class, if you will." Mr. Hall's hand rested briefly on her shoulder, and then he walked away. Linda breathed a sigh of relief. She hadn't cried—yet. She bent over her proofs.

"I'm sorry, Linda, honest."

Linda realized with a start that George was by her desk. "Go away," she hissed between set teeth. "Just go away."

"I didn't have to be nasty." George's voice was low. "I— maybe it's because I had waited."

Linda grabbed her galleys and pushed past him. Her classmates, she knew, were staring at her. Head high, she walked to Mr. Hall's desk and laid the proof before him. "My editorial," she said.

"I've okayed it." Mr. Hall pointed to his initials. "Should go over with the students. You've got a knack with words." He shuffled through the rest of the material. "Looks as though we have a good page," he said, handing the proof back.

Linda's cheeks still felt hot as she returned to her desk. At least George had returned to his side of the room. Maybe Mr. Hall thought she had a knack with words, but that wasn't the only thing she had a knack with. She also had the knack of making herself the most conspicuous fool in Claremar High. Vickie—that's what she'd been trying to tell her, that George already had been asked. Schoolmates, close friends, family—everyone would be aware of her humiliation.

When the dismissal bell rang, Linda waited until the others left before she went to Mr. Hall's desk. "You said—"

"No hurry," he interrupted. "I just wanted to remind you that the *Clarion* staff is expected to have a booth at our carnival. We'd like you to take charge."

Was he just trying to be nice? Sandy, as editor-in-chief, was the natural choice.

"Sandy can't give it the time," Mr. Hall explained, as

if he'd read her doubts. "Besides," he added, "every activity adds to your record."

"Thank you." Linda smiled at Mr. Hall. He was trying so hard to help her be a finalist in the American Field Service program. Maybe next summer she would be in France. "Thank you," she repeated. "I'll really try."

"And, Linda?"

"Yes?"

"Problems have a way of getting solved."

"That's what Dad says. I'll remember." Linda went to her desk and picked up her books. Was Mr. Hall speaking of the carnival booth, or referring to her, personally? She walked past George's desk on her way out. It was neat and tidy, the way George was. *Georgie Porgie, pudding and pie.* The nursery rhyme slipped into her mind. He hadn't made her cry—not quite.

CHAPTER 3

DATE BUREAU

Linda walked home alone, thankful that Beth had practice. She needed to sort out her thoughts. Her dilemma was of her own making. To mention Doug was unthinkable, but omitting him would be omitting her only logical reason for not asking George earlier. Because of Angela the family would know of her humiliation. Would Tim be embarrassed for her?

As her thoughts churned, Linda was hardly aware of the blocks she covered. The late September sun felt good as it warmed her shoulders. The occasional spirals of smoke she saw meant that backyard gardeners were burning leaves. The pungent smoke of eucalyptus and maple leaves was an aroma she wished she could bottle, to sniff at during the other seasons. She shifted her books and half smiled. Maybe, those other seasons, she'd have better luck with dances.

Her home looked deserted as she opened the front door. She stood in the entrance hall a moment, listening. Mom was in the kitchen. "I'm home!" Linda called.

Mom, wiping her hands on a towel, pushed open the kitchen door with her elbow. "Good day? I'm making a banana cake," she continued, without waiting for Linda to answer. "Dad phoned. He was underbid." She smiled ruefully. "We'll barbecue. He'll like that."

"Need any help?"

"Everything's under control," Mom said. "Except— Linda?"

"Yes, Mom?"

"Let's try for a congenial evening. Okay?"

Linda grinned at her mother. *That* was a sly way of saying, *Don't fight with your brothers.* "Okay," she agreed.

Mom looked satisfied. Linda watched her return to the kitchen, and then took the stairs two at a time to her own room. She gave her dress a reproving shake before hanging it in her closet. "A lot of good you did," she told it. She sat at her desk and opened her English text. This morning when she'd looked at the dress she'd still been hopeful. Doug had been so cute, so friendly. Why had he changed? She knew it wasn't another girl, and yet he'd acted as though she hadn't the right to ask. Oh well, thinking about it was no help. It was impossible just to erase the day, but she could try to concentrate on homework.

As she read her assignments Linda was vaguely aware of the twins getting home from Cubs and Tim thumping up the stairs for a shower. Had Angela told him yet? A little later she heard Dad come in. Still later he rapped on her door.

"Supper, princess," he said. "I'm putting on the hamburgers."

"Be right there, Dad." She pushed her books back on the desk. Dad's voice. He hadn't sounded depressed over losing the bid. He—he'd sounded sympathetic. So Dad knew.

27

At first when Linda went down to the patio she thought that the strained atmosphere was because Mom had warned the rest of the family about Dad's bad day. But no, it wasn't that. They'd heard about *her* bad day, and had jointly resolved to pretend that it hadn't happened. At least that's the way it seemed. Conversation seemed so forced.

She watched Tim pour catsup over his hamburger until it dripped from the sides of the bun. He took a bite, then wiped his chin and hands on his napkin. He caught her gaze. "I like catsup," he said.

There was still a dribble of red at the corner of his mouth. Linda looked at it with disgust. "Obviously," she said. Her tone was cutting. "Boys are pigs." She waited for his retort.

"Linda." Mom sounded sympathetic—and reproving. "Pass me the catsup, dear."

Tim had turned to Dad. "Sorry you lost the bid, Dad," he said. "Did it—hurt?"

"Any lost business hurts," Dad explained. "I felt pretty bad for a while. But it's happened before; it'll happen again. The construction business is just that way." He helped himself to potato salad and passed Tim the bowl. "At least we won't be starving," he added. "As a matter of fact, I've a deal cooking now that may put us on easy street. It—well, I can't talk about it yet. It just came in before I left the office."

"Thirds, Dad?" asked Jeff.

Linda watched as Dad served Jeff, and then Tim and Johnny, thirds on the hamburgers. So Dad's bad day had turned into a good day, sort of. Well, there was no way *her* day could be saved. Now conversation lagged again.

Each effort seemed to peter out. It was as if—as if they were all characters in a comic strip, each with a conversational balloon above his head, and Linda would go along popping the balloons, dissolving them into nothing. She half chuckled at the image. *I'll blow up balloons of my own,* she decided.

"You know the annual Claremar carnival?" she asked. "Mr. Hall's appointed me chairman of the *Clarion's* booth."

"Quite an honor," Dad said. "Mr. Hall is a smart man."

"It'll mean work," said Mom.

"That's what I meant about Mr. Hall's being smart," said Dad. "He knows our daughter's the best." He smiled at Linda, and Linda felt she could almost bask in the warmth of his pride.

"I'll have to think of an idea too. What we should have," she added.

"Popcorn's popular," Dad offered.

"I like shooting ducks, like at the beach," said Jeff.

"Or throwing darts at balloons," Johnny cut in.

"All carnivals have those booths. Linda wants hers different," said Tim.

"I wonder." Mom's voice was suddenly dreamy. "The carnivals in our day, Fred . . ."

Linda was going to remind her mother that booths did get outdated when she heard the muted ring of the phone.

"Answer it, Jeff," Dad said. "Tell whoever it is we're at dinner."

"It has to run all day and evening," Linda said. "The booth, I mean."

"If I can help build it," Dad said, "materials, maybe—"

The back door slammed and Jeff was back at his seat at

the table. "Bud," he said. "Call him later, Tim. He said would Dad pick up if his Dad took."

"Make sense," Dad said impatiently. "What are you talking about?"

"The dance. He's trying to figure rides," Johnny explained. "Like this morning, Tim wanted to—" Johnny suddenly clapped his hand over his mouth and looked pleadingly from Linda to Mom. "I forgot, Mom, honest," he said.

Linda felt sudden rage boil in her. "Okay," she said, "now it's in the open. You know, and I know you know. I'm a dud—a creep no one will date for the dance. And I'm sorry you have to be ashamed of me." She swung her legs over the bench. "I'll leave so you can enjoy yourselves more."

"Linda." Dad's voice was stern.

"Let her go, Fred," Mom said quietly. "It's best this way."

"Sure, it's best." Linda flung the words at them. "When I'm gone you can be normal again. You can talk and laugh and have fun. You won't have to have a wake for your socially dead butterfly." Her throat hurt and she swallowed hard. "I'm sorry," she said quietly. "I'm sorry I'm so rude. But please, please, may I be excused?"

"Yes, my dear," Dad agreed. "You may."

Linda shut her bedroom door behind her and flung herself across her bed. She wanted to cry, but now the tears wouldn't come. She looked at her clock. Just twelve hours ago she'd been so hopeful, so anticipating. But now—now she might just as well get to her studies. There was nothing else to do. And if she were going to study, she might as well be comfortable. She changed into her pajamas, fluffed

30

up her pillow, and settled back against it. It was still light outside—daylight saving. She tried to concentrate on her history assignment. So many "causes" in those early American days, and people had been so dedicated. Causes, her teacher had said, were built on basic principles of human dignity. He might have added that nowadays they thrived in cities and never seemed to reach you in the suburbs. What would it be like, she wondered, to have a cause? She heard a rap on her door.

"Come in!" she called.

Johnny and Jeff shuffled into the room. They looked embarrassed as they stood near the door.

"Well?"

They both squirmed uncomfortably. "We thought," Jeff began, "that maybe—"

"We got this idea," Johnny cut in. "We know a guy. He's good. He's rec director."

"You'd probably think he's handsome, even. He's in college, though," Jeff said.

"What are you talking about?"

"We thought maybe we could ask him," Jeff said. "It's an idea."

"Ask who what?"

"Gee, Linda, ask the rec guy to take you to the dance," Johnny said. "I mean, we thought, well—"

Linda looked at her twin brothers. They were so uncomfortable and were trying so hard.

"George stinks," Jeff said. "We hate him."

"It was my fault, really. I waited too long."

"We already told this guy a long time ago that we have

a cute sister," Johnny said. "He even told us he'd like to meet you."

Linda's smile felt wobbly as she faced her brothers. "Someday," she said, "someday I'll be glad to meet him. But not for the dance. It's all right. Really."

"You sure?" Jeff looked doubtful.

"We wouldn't mind asking," Johnny said.

"I'm sure."

Now the twins looked as though they wanted to escape, only they didn't know how to leave. "I've—I've homework," Linda said softly. "Okay?"

"Okay." They started out of the room. Jeff turned back at the door. "You're no dud," he said firmly. "So there." He gave her a broad wink.

Linda looked at her history book again, but the words blurred. The tears in her eyes weren't sad tears. They were— The twins were darlings, even if they were boys. It must have taken tremendous effort on their part even to make the offer. She could imagine how they'd squirm with the rec director if she'd agreed. Yet, for her . . .

"Hey, sis!" Tim's loud knock accompanied his call. "Come in."

"Boy, you're sure in bed early," he said as he stepped uneasily into her room. Girls' rooms, he claimed, were so fussy, they made him uncomfortable. He looked it now as he put his hands in his pockets and took them out again. "I was thinking," he began. His voice faded; then he squared his shoulders and started again. "I was thinking— well, Bud and I, we know lots of guys who aren't freshmen, and—" He looked helplessly at Linda. "What I mean is, if we called around, maybe, tonight, why then—"

"You mean maybe you could fix me up for the Fall Frolic?"

"Yeah—yeah, that's it." Tim's face showed relief at her help. "We know some pretty good guys."

"Thanks for trying, Tim." Linda spoke the words softly. "But no, I goofed. Time ran out on me. I—it's all my fault. And—"

"But honest, sis, I'll bet lots of guys wished you'd asked them."

"But I didn't. And now it's too late." She closed her history book and propped it against her knees. "Don't feel bad. I won't—I won't go into a tail spin. After all, it's just a dance."

"You're sure you don't want Bud and me to fix you up with a date?"

"I'm sure." Linda looked at her brother. "But thanks for trying, for thinking about me."

"Look, sis"—Tim faced his sister squarely—"you're no dud, you know. You're even sort of cute."

"Thanks, Tim. Thanks—for everything."

"Okay, then." Tim backed toward the door. "I just thought . . ."

"I know." Linda watched Tim leave the room. The relief on his face was unmistakable. Golly, such loyalty. She really must have upset the family. She heard new footsteps on the stairway. Mom or Dad? She grinned as she heard Dad's voice.

"Come in!" she called. "Hi, Dad. And suggestions?"

"Eh?" Dad blinked his surprise. "Suggestions? I just wanted to say that one of the fellows working for me

33

has a son, a senior. Goes to a different school. I thought, maybe . . ."

"Dad." Linda felt as if her grin were stretched from ear to ear. This was getting comical. "I—I don't have to go to the dance. I don't even care as much now. I goofed, I missed out. I waited too long."

"He'd be proud to go with you," Dad said. "Any boy would. That George ought to have his head examined. You're no dud; you—"

Linda laughed. "I'm a real social butterfly," she said. "Only this time I got my wings crossed." She held out her hand. "Honest, Dad, I don't mind any more—at least, not as much."

"You're sure?" Dad sat on the edge of the bed and held her hand. "I wouldn't mind," he insisted. "I just don't want you unhappy. That's what counts."

"I'm sure."

Dad stood up. "Okay, princess." He leaned over and kissed her. "I'm proud of you," he added.

Maybe, Linda reflected as Dad left, being the only girl had advantages. She was always sure, for instance, of Dad's approval and sympathy. He acted as if she really were a princess. She opened her book again and started to read. Mom should be coming in any minute now. Surely *she'd* take a turn. Linda listened a few minutes, expectantly, and then, reluctantly, turned her full attention to Shays' Rebellion. She'd completed history and had done her French translations before she heard Mom.

"I brought you dessert," said Mom. "And an idea."

"Who?" Linda asked.

"You mean *what*," Mom corrected. "We thought it absolutely wonderful. We actually wore out three Miss Townsends. And we almost made the most money."

"Hmm?"

"A Swat-the-Faculty booth," Mom explained. "You make dummies, teacher dummies. I've often wondered if Miss Townsend knew how popular—or, more accurately, how *un*popular she was."

"Swat the faculty." Linda repeated the words. It sounded great. Mr. Marsh—Mr. Hill—would they approve? "I can see it now," Linda said between mouthfuls of cake.

"Good." Mom smiled down at Linda. "I'll think of all the details I can. Now—give me your plate and glass."

Linda took a final swallow of milk. "Know why I thought you came up? I thought you were coming to tell me about a date you could get me."

"A date? To the dance?" Mom shook her head. "Hardly—at least not under these circumstances."

"George was already asked."

Mom nodded. "I know. He must have felt bad, turning you down. He called before supper. I didn't know what he was talking about at first, but he finally explained."

"I—I didn't really want to take him. I—I asked another boy first."

"And he'd been asked?"

"Mom, he was so embarrassing. He just said no without a reason. I kept wondering all day who'd heard him. Just, 'Sorry, no,' and I'm sure he hadn't been asked before." Linda's cheeks felt hot. "Mom, it was so—so humiliating."

"Maybe he couldn't explain. What if he didn't know how to dance, maybe? Don't you think he'd be too embarrassed to explain that?"

Linda looked doubtful. Somehow Doug didn't look like the type who couldn't dance.

"I know this is preachy, Linda," Mom said, "but I have one suggestion."

"Yes?"

"Don't procrastinate. You did 'put off.' Let this be a lesson."

Linda watched Mom leave the room. Today *had* been a lesson. She'd learned a lot. Somehow she was reminded of Dr. Seuss's elephant who meant what he said and said what he meant. Her family was faithful, one hundred per cent.

CHAPTER 4

FOUR-WHEEL BRAKES

What a difference two short weeks could make! Linda leaned against the window sill of the deserted journalism room and gazed across the sunlit campus. Friday. School was out for the weekend. Tonight Claremar's varsity would play its first league game—a home game too. And Mary Lou was giving a pre-game potluck supper—Mary Lou said she expected about thirty girls. Funny, it seemed so good to be alive when only two Fridays ago she'd stayed home, heartsick, humiliated, feeling unwanted, while her friends had a wonderful time at the Fall Frolic.

"Almost through, miss?"

Linda turned from the window. Time for the custodian to clean the room already? She hadn't finished reading through the Hi-Jinks copy but had been daydreaming instead.

"I'll finish in a jiffy," she promised as she sat at her desk. She tackled the copy with vigor. This was something else to be enthusiastic about—the Hi-Jinks, Claremar's carnival. She hoped it would go over big. And the money it raised would help to pay for the Claremar exchange students' expenses. Maybe—just maybe— Imagine spending a summer in France!

In a matter of minutes Linda was finished. She cleared

her desk and picked up the layout for the Hi-Jinks hand-bills. Now a trip to the Star printing shop. On the way to her locker she passed the custodian. "Sorry I kept you waiting."

"That's okay." The custodian smiled as he shouldered his large broom. "Just want to be through in plenty of time so I get to the game tonight. Great team this year."

Linda nodded her agreement. The local sports writers were predicting great things for Claremar's varsity, before they'd even played their first game. And—just as the custodian was hurrying so he could get to the game—so, she bet, were most of the town's residents. It was fun to live in a town that took its football team seriously.

She hurried to the student parking lot. She had so many things to do: fix the salad, wash her hair . . . She felt keyed up, excited. How must the football team feel? Was Beth nervous? She'd been good at the noon rally. Linda opened the car door and slid behind the wheel. Now that she was a junior, she was allowed the family car one day a week. Lucky today was the day.

The drive to the printshop was short, but Linda couldn't find a parking place anywhere near it, so she drove around the block and parked off the main street. The tiny front office of the Star Printers felt like an oven when Linda walked in.

Mr. Benning peered out from the back room. "Ah, Linda," he said, "bring the copy here. The missus has gone home already." He peered through thick lenses at the layout she placed on the long table. "Hi-Jinks," he read.

"You'd better come," Linda said. "Look." She ran her finger down a list. "Here's the *Clarion* booth—Swat-the-Faculty." She wished there were some way to make that particular booth stand out on the handbill. Mom's suggestion had met with Mr. Hall's hearty approval and Mr. Marsh had given his okay.

"The missus and I—we'll go." Mr. Benning beamed at her. "You going to the game tonight?"

"I guess just about everybody's going."

"A good team. That Steve Atkins, he's a great player, maybe."

"He'll be in the starting line-up."

"If he plays in all the games, we'll be champs. Maybe he'll make All-Star."

"That would be great. He—" Linda closed her mouth. She'd almost told Mr. Benning that her best friend, Beth, had actually dated Steve. *Don't be a name dropper*, she scolded herself.

Mr. Benning turned back to the copy. Linda explained some of her type markings, then started to leave.

"A minute, Linda." Mr. Benning paused as if searching for words. "Your editorials," he said slowly, "the missus and I, we read them." He took off his glasses and wiped them on his handkerchief. "We think it time, maybe, you write on responsibility—straight thinking."

Linda looked at him in amazement. It was not like Mr. Benning to make a suggestion like this.

"Things are happening," he continued, "things that are not right for Claremar. A little roughhouse, a few fights, some drinking, driving too fast . . ." He put his glasses back on and peered at her owlishly. "Straws in the wind, maybe."

"Not—not Claremar High kids," Linda protested. "You don't mean us."

"Claremar High kids, yes," he said emphatically. "The small triumph—sometimes it comes too fast to be used well. A little importance goes to the head. Our good life—perhaps it is too easy." Mr. Benning looked grim. "A word in time, like a stitch in time . . ." He left his sentence unfinished, dangling between them.

"I'll—I'll think about it."

"It is good. You use your brain." He turned away and Linda knew she was now dismissed.

An editorial on responsibility, straight thinking? Linda gave a mental shrug. Beth, Vickie and Mary Lou already thought Linda was too preachy, too "too." She walked down the street to her car. Claremar High was wonderful. The kids were the greatest. Sure, there were a few—there'd have to be in a school of fifteen hundred kids—who were troublemakers—boys who were just marking time until they could quit. And some girls dropped out to get married—because they grew up too fast. But Mr. Benning hadn't spoken as if he meant these. "A little importance . . ." He'd hinted that the "regular" ones were heading for trouble. Linda felt anxious to get home, to make the salad for Mary Lou's potluck supper, to wash her hair for the game, to do things that would make her forget Mr. Benning's dour words.

She crossed the street hurriedly, opened the car door and slid in. As she did, a piece of paper was blown out onto the sidewalk. She reached down to pick it up but a playful breeze scudded it out of reach. She got out and it was within an inch of her grasp when the breeze whisked it into the street. Now it lay face up, covered with her notes. She darted toward it and stamped her foot on it just as she heard the blare of a horn and screech of brakes. She jumped back instinctively. A car, a decrepit old jalopy, had stopped within inches of where she'd stood. She looked toward the driver to apologize, and saw Doug Johnson's white, angry face as he leaned out the window.

"Look where you're going!" he shouted. "I could have—"

Another car stopped behind him, and the driver leaned impatiently on his horn. Doug shifted gears and drove off.

Linda gritted her teeth. He'd almost hit her, then yelled at her. She picked up the paper, got back in the car, and started off for home. That Doug Johnson! If only she'd answered back!

She turned into her driveway, where Johnny and Jeff were hard at work watering the lawn and themselves.

"Come play with us!" called Jeff.

The spraying water looked cool and refreshing. If she made the salad and washed her hair quickly . . . "I will," she said.

"Promise?" asked Johnny.

"I promise."

She hurried to her room, deposited her books, and changed into shorts, then went back downstairs and to the kitchen. "I'm home, Mom," she said as she pushed open the door.

"Have a good day?" Mom looked up from her cookies. "Salad fixings are in the refrigerator," she continued, without waiting for Linda to answer. "Make two bowls, okay? We'll have some for our dinner too."

"Okay." With quick, deft movements, Linda got to work.

"Maybe," she said as her mother popped a batch of cookies into the oven, "maybe I'll skip the green onions. There's a dance at the rec center after the game, you know."

"Cut up a few on ours," Mom said. "We don't have to be polite."

Except for the dressing, the salads were finished. Linda covered them and placed them on refrigerator shelves. "Okay if I make green goddess dressing?" she asked. "It's so special."

"Well . . ." Mom hesitated. "Oh, all right. But you'll have to buy sour cream. As Dad took the train to the city today, I want you to pick him up at the depot. Get it then. Put everything else in the blender now."

Linda set the blender on its stand and measured in the ingredients. All ready except for the sour cream. She placed the top on the blender and picked up the leftover lemon half. She felt her lips pucker as she bit into it. Tim claimed she was crazy, the way she ate lemons.

"You look sour." Mom slipped a pan of cookies into the oven as she spoke.

Linda chuckled. "I'm not," she said. Then her face sobered. "Mr. Benning was, though. He thinks Claremar kids are wild."

"Some are."

"He didn't mean *those*, the dumb ones, or the ones who don't count. He meant the regulars." Linda bit off another piece of rind.

"Linda Chapin. *You* sound like a snob."

"You're agreeing with Mr. Benning?"

"I'm questioning how you decide who counts."

"Background, I guess." Linda felt confused. Mom

42

sounded so belligerent, so serious. "Some kids have good families, some don't."

"If you mean by 'good' a family who cares, you're safe." Mom brushed back a wisp of hair. "But if you're thinking of 'good' addresses—" Mom hesitated, then went on. "Remember the party this summer, the one you girls left early because you didn't like it? It became a brawl. The police were called?"

"Yes, but—"

"Weren't the guests your so-called regulars?"

"Nobody really got in trouble. Nobody pressed charges."

"It's a bit difficult to press charges against friends," Mom said. "Or the children of friends."

"But that was just one little party," Linda defended.

"It gives Mr. Benning a point, and you something to think about. Remember, Linda, your dad always says that having too much can be as difficult as not having enough."

"Mr. Benning calls it 'our good life.'"

"So it is, make no mistake about that. But for a few it is too much, too soon, and they become bored. And for both rich or poor, boredom is a dangerous thing. There's a world of truth to the old saw about Satan and idle hands." Mom's eyes were pleadingly serious. "Do you get my point, Linda? Boredom is an insidious disease."

"Yes, but—"

"But what?"

"Well, Mr. Benning also talked about importance, or rather, a *little* importance going to the head, he called it."

"Surely you see that. A false sense of self-importance must hit all of us at some time. Our histories are full of glaring examples of indispensables who were actually

43

easily expendable. Just remember, self-delusion and boredom are distinctly separate feelings independent of each other, and— Oh, dear—" Mom sniffled, then made a dash for the oven.

Linda surveyed the sheet of sorry-looking charred disks. "I'm sorry, Mom. I should have helped you remember."

"My own fault. Baking and—and lecturing don't mix. At least this was the last batch." Mom scraped the burned mess into the garbage. "And my last lecture of the day," she added. "I promise."

"Thanks, Mom. I mean I'll—"

"Hey, sis, when you coming out?" Linda couldn't tell whether it was Jeff or Johnny who called.

"I promised the twins to get my feet wet," she explained. "They're playing with the hose." The idea seemed so childish, *was* so childish after Mom's serious talk, that Linda felt embarrassed.

Mom gave a quizzical laugh. "Off with you, youngster," she said. "And take these to your brothers." She gave Linda a handful of oatmeal cookies.

"Hurry," said Jeff as Linda walked out on the sidewalk. "The lawn's almost drowned."

"Maybe another day." Linda divided the cookies between the boys.

"Uh-uh," Johnny mumbled with his mouth full. "You promised."

"We want to play hurdles," added Jeff.

The hot pavement, the wet grass, the spray from the hose suddenly looked good. Linda capitulated. "Okay." She slipped off her shoes and held the hose as Jeff and Johnny leaped over the stream of water. They seemed so pleased

44

when they missed and were soaked. It had been a long time since she'd played this game.

"Your turn," Jeff announced.

"Well—" Linda hesitated only a minute.

Jeff lowered the spray for her first few trial leaps. He started inching it up. Johnny egged her on with raucous "rahs." This was fun—kid stuff, but fun. She was almost as good as the twins. "Once more, and I'll have to quit," she said, laughing. Just as she leaped, she caught sight of a car pulling to the curb. Tim. He'd got a ride home from football practice.

"That a girl, sis!" Tim called.

Linda stopped, aghast. It was Doug's jalopy—Tim in Doug's jalopy. She took a quick step backward, into the full force of the spray. She was drenched. She turned and ran for the house. Slamming the door behind her, she cut off the shouts of laughter. She leaned against the door for a minute and pushed her wet hair out of her eyes. The door pushed open against her as Tim and the twins burst in.

"Some show, sis," Tim sputtered, as though he couldn't get his breath. "Some show for a junior."

"You're so drippy," said Johnny.

"Drip, drip, drippy," added Jeff. "A drippy sister."

Without a word Linda turned and ran up the stairs. Their laughter followed her. "Hey, sis," Tim called, "Doug said he was glad he gave me a ride home—any time, he said, for a show like that! Know what else he said?" Tim broke off to laugh. "He said to watch where you're going, or else get four-wheel brakes."

CHAPTER 5

ALL FOR ONE

By the time Linda was ready to pick up her father she had simmered down. Brothers were brats, for a fact. But Tim could have been furious with embarrassment at her childish play. Instead he'd thought her funny. And Doug —well, no one was even aware she knew him. To see him away from school twice in one day was completely unexpected, especially since they took pains to avoid each other ever since she'd asked him to the dance. At least *she* took pains to avoid *him,* that was for sure.

She checked her reflection in the mirror. No signs of her ridiculous soaking since she'd shampooed and showered. She looked properly tidy but wished she looked glamorous. When she stopped at the kitchen her three brothers looked at her with teasing grins but said nothing. "Need anything, Mom?" she asked.

"Just the sour cream," Mom answered.

Traffic was heavy near the depot. Linda pulled into a space in the parking lot and switched off the engine. The sleek red convertible two cars away looked familiar. So did the boy behind the wheel. Steve Atkins. But shouldn't he be home relaxing before a game?

The train ground to a stop, and the passengers came crowding off the steps. Dad was in earnest conversation with

46

another man. Linda honked and waved. He returned her greeting and continued talking. They stopped by the convertible and Linda saw Dad shake hands with Steve. A minute later, Steve, with the man beside him, was backing out, and Dad was walking toward her.

"Sorry to keep you waiting, princess," Dad said. "But it was business." He pulled the door shut.

"Business?"

"Not young Atkins," Dad explained. "That was pleasure. He's in the starting line-up tonight, you know. Captain of the team too. Right?"

"Right." Linda backed out and became a part of the moving traffic.

"Atkins is sure proud of that boy. During our discussions I'd have the feeling Mr. Atkins wasn't with me, and, sure enough, he'd start talking about Steve and football."

"What discussions, Dad?"

"Business, princess, Mr. Atkins has some pretty big plans, and I hope to be in on them. I spent most of the day with him, checking out his ideas."

Dad working with Mr. Atkins? She knew he owned a big hotel in the city, but Dad wasn't a remodeling man, and Claremar hardly seemed the place for a big hotel. She braked to a stop in front of the market. "For the potluck," she said. "I'll just be a minute."

She was just getting back into the car when she heard the squeal of tires and looked up to see Steve make an illegal U turn. Dad had a *thing* about teen-age drivers, and she waited for his outburst, but as the car passed theirs he merely leaned across her. "See you at the game!" he called.

47

"We'll keep our eyes on seventy-seven." Mr. Atkins clapped Steve across the shoulders.

Dad chuckled. "A real character," he said as he relaxed against the seat. "A determined winner."

Linda glanced at her father. Was he talking about Steve —or his dad?

The wait until it was time to go to Mary Lou's seemed endless. Now as Linda rang the bell there was so much noise that she wondered if she were late. She turned and waved at Dad.

"Have fun, princess!" he called. "See you at the game, maybe."

The door opened, and Linda elbowed her way through the mass of girls to the tune of cheery "hi's" and placed her salad on the table among the other foods.

"Isn't it perf?" Mary Lou was beaming. "Isn't it just perf?"

Linda grinned broadly. The excitement and enthusiasm were contagious. "Absolutely perf," she agreed.

Then they were engulfed by girls placing their "specials" on the table, and Linda went in search of Beth. She found her sitting in a corner in the living room, alone and looking scared.

"Beth," she said softly. "Is something wrong?"

Beth looked up, starry-eyed. Steve's Block C sweater hung from her shoulders, almost hiding her blue, pleated cheerleading skirt in its bigness. "No," she said, and her voice was only a whisper. "Only—only everything is so wonderful, so perfect, I'm—I'm scared."

"You need food." Linda pulled Beth to her feet. "Let's

48

join the mob." Linda felt ravenous as they got in line. She wanted some of everything.

"Mock ravioli," said one proud contributor of a casserole as Linda helped herself. Linda glanced quickly at her salad bowl and noted that its contents were almost depleted. The Drapers, Mary Lou's parents, stood at the far end of the table, filling milk glasses and passing out hunks of savory hot French bread.

"Cheese or herb?" asked Mr. Draper.

"Both, please." Linda added them to the mountain of food on her plate. She and Beth found an unoccupied corner and were joined by Vickie and Mary Lou. Conversation swarmed around them like the buzz of bees until they almost had to yell at each other to be heard. Steve's name was in the air constantly and Beth grinned fatuously at each mention of him. Linda frowned. It wasn't like Beth to go overboard for a boy. But she'd been like this, more or less, ever since the Fall Frolic. Linda hoped Steve reciprocated.

"Linda?"

"Huh?"

"You're daydreaming. Snap out of it." Vickie's voice was sharp. "I said, I'm taking the cheerleaders to the game now. You want to come along?"

Linda looked at Mary Lou.

"I—I'll get a ride in the last car—or come with my parents," Mary Lou said. "You go ahead and save me a seat."

"Okay," Linda picked up her empty plate and reached for Beth's. "You didn't eat," she scolded.

49

"I can't, I— What if I don't lead the yells right or something?"

"Don't be silly!" Linda stacked the plates and took them to the kitchen before saying her good-bys.

The glare of the floodlights on the football field made it almost as bright as day as Linda followed Vickie to the rooting section. The bleachers were filling fast. Claremar's Bobcats were drawing a record crowd tonight. Across the way Westhaven wasn't faring too badly either. Pretty soon there wouldn't be an empty seat. She looked at her program, Mr. Benning's printing job. She hoped that he and his wife had found good seats. Her parents, the twins, and Tim—were they here yet? She looked over at the sea of faces in the general section. She saw Mr. Atkins and his wife, but couldn't find her own family. Maybe Tim was already in the rooting section. She craned her neck and looked up, then felt Mary Lou squeeze in beside her.

"It's packed, jammed," Mary Lou murmured. "Look, here come the bands."

Westhaven's band marched onto the field in orderly fashion, the red and gold uniforms gleaming under floodlights. The crowd cheered. Then came Claremar's band, looking almost mechanized in its precise march onto the field. Linda cheered wildly with the rest. Now the teams came on the field—the Westhaven Webfeet and Claremar's Bobcats. The roar from the crowd made the bleachers quiver. The cheerleaders were silencing the crowd, and the people rose up en masse for the raising of the flag as the bands played "The Star-Spangled Banner." Linda's eyes felt wet and she swallowed hard as the bands marched off the field and the two teams limbered up with trial passing and kicking. Everything looked so new, so shining, so untouched, like a brand-new page. What would be written on it? Victory for the Bobcats, she hoped. Three years in a row they'd been edged out of first place—infuriating for a football town. Maybe, now—

Westhaven was kicking, Claremar receiving. The announcer gave the line-up—*George*, Linda recognized. ". . . Steve Atkins, seventy-seven . . ." He droned on and on.

"I'm—I'm goose-pimply," said Mary Lou.

Linda could feel her own scalp prickle as the whistle blew, the drums rolled, and Westhaven moved down the field. The kick was a beaut! It went high, crossing the field at an angle and dropped down on the twelve-yard line, then bounced out of bounds.

"Oh, no," groaned Vickie. "What a beginning."

"Claremar's ball on their own twelve. First down, ten to go." George's voice was almost a monotone.

Linda felt her gaze riveted to the field as the Bobcats huddled, went into formation.

"A run around left end . . . gain of about three yards . . ."

Back in formation again. Now Steve faded back to pass. The receiver was in the clear. Linda couldn't catch her breath. Steve pivoted slightly; then, instead of passing, he started down the field. He was going to be smeared! But no. He was off—yard after yard after yard.

"Touchdown! A touchdown!" George's voice cracked with excitement.

Pandemonium broke loose.

"What a play!" Mary Lou gasped. "Look at Beth."

Beth, as she tried with the others to lead an organized

51

yell, looked as though the excitement was almost too much for her. Then she was racing with the other leaders to the end zone. There the girls fell to their knees like handmaidens imploring the favor of a mythical god.

"Bob Brown, number thirty-five, trying for the extra point . . ."

The ball sailed smoothly between the goal posts. The score stood at 7 to 0 in the first few minutes of play.

Vickie let go of Linda's arm as the three girls sat down. Linda heard their long, quavering sighs and released her own pent-up breath. The defense team lined up. Bob Brown was kicking. The crowd stood up, tense, waiting.

Bob's kick was good, but not as good as the Webfoot's. The ball was put into play on Westhaven's twenty-five yard line. With sustained effort, the Webfeet drove deep into Claremar's territory. Inch by inch, foot by foot, yard by yard, down by down, they beat the Claremar defense back. Twice it looked as if they'd lost the ball on downs, but measuring proved that they made it a first by inches. Near the end of the first quarter they made a first down on Claremar's seven.

"Hold that line, hold that line!" chanted Claremar rooters.

"We want a touchdown, we want a touchdown!" Westhaven rooters screamed.

The Bobcats' line held for two downs; then the Webfoot quarterback fumbled and Claremar recovered as the gun went off. Linda felt pity for the boy who fumbled even as she felt relief that it was Claremar's ball.

The teams changed goals. Linda was glad that Dad had insisted his family know their football. She could understand so much of what was happening during plays.

The Bobcats made first down by sheer push. Then Linda saw a setup for a pass. She watched as Steve hung onto the ball instead. What a dangerous chance to take! Again he took off down the field, and again the excellent blocking of his teammates got him into the clear. He raced to another touchdown. Another conversion, and the score stood at Claremar 14, Westhaven 0. Steve—he was terrific! With the second score against them, the Webfeet seemed to come unglued. The Bobcats were just too good.

During the third quarter Linda noted ruefully that Steve was making sensational plays rather than sound ones. He was showing off, playing more for Steve than for Claremar. And his teammates were helping. Dad must be boiling if he was "keeping his eye on seventy-seven." How many times had he lectured Tim, and even the twins, on the importance of a team's existence as a whole, with individual players mere interlocking parts. He wouldn't approve of this; the Bobcats were an auxiliary to Steve's maneuvers. And why weren't the bench warmers getting a chance at substitution with the score so one-sided? When the final gun went off, the score stood Steve Atkins, 32, Westhaven, 0.

The rooting section was always first to empty. As the girls milled toward the exit Linda saw her parents with Mr. and Mrs. Atkins. Dad beckoned her to join them.

"See you at the car," she told Vickie and Mary Lou.

"Our daughter, Linda," Dad said proudly.

Mrs. Atkins made a barely audible acknowledgment. Her husband made up for it in volume. He grinned at Linda like a Cheshire cat, his heavy jowls bulging over his collar. "Well," he said, "some game! My Steve, he sure showed them, didn't he, kid?"

"The first game that counts," said Linda. "And we won."

"We won?" Mr. Atkins snorted. *"Steve* won. It was his game, all the way."

Linda felt herself bristle. Westhaven's zero reflected the Bobcats' strong defense. The blockers and tacklers, hadn't they helped plenty?

"He played a spectacular game," Dad said. "Agreed, Linda?"

"Sure—if you like spectacles." Linda caught her father's sharp glance of disapproval. Yet surely he knew even better than she the kind of game Steve had played. Was he condoning it?

"Our Steve will make All-Star. Nothing can stop him." Mr. Atkins' set face reflected the determination of his words.

Tim bounded up the bleachers, the twins right behind him, hero worship written on their faces. Linda wanted to escape. "I've got to go," she said. "My friends are waiting. 'By." She turned away.

"Be home by twelve-thirty," Mom reminded her.

As Linda joined the crowd heading for the exit she felt disturbed. Was she the only one who thought the victory flat? Tonight it had been all for one, all for Steve. It should have been one for all. And Dad, when she left, had looked *angry*. At her?

CHAPTER 6

BIG BUSINESS

Linda walked slowly to the car. She couldn't have hurried if she'd wanted to. The street was a bedlam of people and cars. The girls weren't waiting, as she'd expected. She looked around, then decided to sit behind the wheel. Traffic cleared, the floodlights went out on the field. Where were Vickie and Mary Lou? Had they misunderstood?

A crowd of students rounded the corner, and she saw Vickie, Beth, and Mary Lou break away and come toward the car.

"You missed it," said Mary Lou. "We serenaded the team."

"Let's walk to the dance," said Vickie. "I'll never find a place to park there."

Linda fell into step with Beth. "You look unhappy," Beth said. "What's the matter?"

Linda shrugged. "Nothing really, except I think my dad's annoyed with me."

"Why?"

"It's too involved." Linda smiled at Beth. "Maybe I just take things too seriously."

"Nobody should take things too seriously. Not tonight." Beth twirled, little-girl fashion. "Everything's just too perfect."

"You're going to get dizzy." Vickie laughed as she took hold of Beth's arm and made her stop. "Let's get to the dance before all the males are snagged."

A few hundred others had the same idea, Linda decided. When they reached the rec center, it was mobbed.

By mutual agreement and through experience, the four girls queued together as they gained the doorway and then the dance floor. They stood on the sidelines, not too far from the main entrance to see who was coming, not too near to get themselves stepped on.

Procedure at a post-game rec dance followed a pattern. Since it was strictly stag, it was a catch-as-catch-can affair. Long ago Mom and Dad had explained to Linda that standing in a large group of girls was committing social suicide. Few boys had nerve enough to extricate a girl from a group of chattering magpies. So the idea was to stand in groups of three or four. If, by some twist of fate, you discovered yourself alone, you'd better get friendly with some girl group fast. Otherwise it was as though you had three feet or used the wrong kind of soap.

You smiled prettily. You looked interested—but not too interested—in the subject you and your friends were discussing. You put your best foot forward and hoped that your lipstick was on right and your slip wasn't showing. Groups of boys strolled by every few minutes, and they looked at you as if they were judging livestock at the county fair. And if you were lucky, one of them would ask you to dance.

Beth and Vickie were always asked first, then Mary Lou and Linda. Tonight it was a tossup. Something—winning the game, maybe, or the blare from the record player, or just because it was a perfect autumn evening—gave the boys impetus. Very few wallflowers decorated the sidelines.

After Steve and the rest of the team came in, Beth danced exclusively with him. They were stopped frequently as others slapped Steve on the back and congratulated him. Beth, on her private cloud nine, looked up at Steve with adoring eyes, taking each word of praise as a personal compliment.

Occasionally Linda bumped into Tim and Angela. Each time Tim arched his eyebrows, winked, and grinned. Apparently having a big sister at a dance wasn't cramping his style.

George, who had been a frequent partner at rec dances prior to the Fall Frolic, asked her to dance only once.

"Great game," he said, leading her onto the floor.

"You did a great job announcing," she said warmly.

Now there was silence between them and Linda searched frantically for something to say. "I took the Hi-Jinks copy in today," she said finally. "And our booth should be pretty good."

"That reminds me," George said. "Shouldn't we be posting the finalists in the American Field Service soon? Hope your name's on the list." He swung Linda into an intricate step, and they collided with another couple. "Sorry," he murmured, then added, "Great game, Steve." He turned back to Linda. "Beth's got herself a hero."

"Is that how you're reporting it? That Steve's a hero?"

"In so many words, yes."

"Then you're not mentioning the second half, I guess."

"What are you getting at, Linda? What's the point you're trying to make?"

"That Steve played bad football the last half. He played for himself only."

"Wow, that's a pretty harsh statement, and maybe you'd better not spread that kind of sentiment around. I mean, Westhaven was beaten the first half. They didn't have a chance. And if Steve did show off a bit, the town loved it, the school loved it—and the way the Bobcats set him up, they loved it too. And that's the way I'll write it."

"Even though—"

"Even though *nothing*. Face facts, Linda. You want something, you work for it. You don't let things get in your way. Claremar wants the championship. Steve wants to make All-Star, get a football scholarship—"

"A scholarship?" Linda interrupted. "With his money?"

"In his case, for prestige." George sounded annoyed. "Maybe there was a scout out in the stands—who knows? Ambitions have price tags, you know. And if you want them, you pay. That's life."

"You sound ruthless, as if maybe ideals don't count."

"Just practical."

This George, Linda didn't know very well. She was glad when the dance ended. She knew it was *their* last dance together.

U. S. History, row 3, seat 2, came up to her. "Smile," he said, "and I'll dance with you."

She smiled and continued to smile at her various partners until the last record was played and the dance ended.

As Linda, Vickie and Mary Lou crowded out the door, Linda saw Beth and Steve waiting for them.

"Steve's driving me home, okay?" Beth asked.

"Sure," said Mary Lou. "Why not?"

"You can't." Linda regretted her role as she spoke up. "Our rules, remember? Our mothers—"

"This is different," Vickie interrupted.

"Rules are rules," Linda said desperately.

"Okay, Simon Legree." Steve was laughing at her. "Next time, Beth."

The girls walked toward the car in silence.

"You sure wouldn't have stopped me," Mary Lou said finally.

"I'm sorry, Beth," Linda apologized. "But rules are . . ."

"Rules," Beth said firmly. "Don't worry. I'm not mad."

Linda looked at Beth gratefully. When it came to a matter of principle Beth always stuck by her. She was a wonderful best friend.

As they got in the car Beth slipped on Steve's sweater and snuggled down in it. "He told me to keep it for a while," she said happily.

Vickie started the motor and let it run for a minute. Just as she was about to pull out from the curb they heard a car clatter down the street. It shuddered to a stop beside them. *Doug.*

He leaned out the window. "Who won?" he called.

"We did!" Vickie yelled back. "Thirty-two to nothing!"

"Great." His glance seemed to catch Linda's and she turned her head. He called something else and drove off.

"What did he say?" asked Beth. "I didn't catch it."

"I'm not sure." Vickie sounded puzzled. "I thought he said, 'Good night, water baby.'"

"It couldn't have been that," Mary Lou said. "That doesn't make sense."

Linda felt her face redden. Doug was impossible!

"Too bad he's a nobody. He's sort of cute." Vickie started to pull out, then stopped short. Steve's red convertible shot by, its horn blaring. He took the corner with tires screeching and his carload of friends yelling.

"Oh, no," groaned Beth as they saw a police car shoot after it. "See what happens, Vickie."

Two blocks down they saw the convertible. Steve was talking to the police officer.

"How horrible." Beth leaned forward to look out the window. "A ticket ruins everything."

As they watched, the officer slapped Steve across the shoulders, pocketed his book, and walked back to the patrol car.

"He didn't get a ticket," Vickie marveled. "Did you see that?"

"It's because he's a hero," Beth said. "The police know that."

Was that the reason? Linda wondered as the cars drove off. She was still wondering when they arrived at her home. She let herself in the front door quietly and then saw the light go on in her parents' room.

"Linda," Dad called, "in here." Linda walked into the room. Dad's eyes were steely. "Why?" he asked. "Why did you do that to me?"

"Do what?"

"Don't be stupid too, Linda. Surely you realized the spot your rudeness put me in." He sighed. "I even told you earlier that Mr. Atkins and I have a deal pending, didn't I?"

Linda nodded.

"Maybe I shouldn't have bragged about my family, but

I did. And then, tonight, I called to you because I wanted the Atkinses to meet my daughter."

"If I disappointed you . . ." Linda started to say.

"You did," Dad said flatly. "He wanted to hear his son praised. Surely you sensed that. But you chose to ignore him. And when I cued you in . . ." He paused. "A man should be able to count on his family."

"You mean, Dad," Linda said carefully, "that I'm to be charming and sweet *no matter what* when I meet your business associates?"

"When you meet anyone, yes."

"I'm sorry I was such a failure." Linda's voice was edged with tears. "But now I know the rules." Her voice broke and she left the room abruptly.

"Linda." Her mother's voice was furious, but Linda didn't turn back. Somehow, it seemed, Dad and George held the same view on deals and ideals. The thought was a bitter one.

CHAPTER 7

A IS FOR ATKINS

The house seemed unnaturally quiet when Linda awoke in the morning. She glanced at the clock. She'd slept so late! She slipped on her bathrobe and hurried downstairs. A note propped against the toaster told her that Mom and Dad were shopping. Johnny and Jeff had scrawled across the bottom that they were at the park. Tim obviously was out too, only he hadn't bothered to say where.

Mom usually insisted that everyone "rise and shine" on Saturdays. Had she let Linda sleep because she and Dad didn't want to see her? Linda wandered from room to room, feeling lonely and rejected. Last night Dad had been cross, and she had been nasty. It had taken her a long time to go to sleep, trying to think things out. She'd heard Tim come in noisily, go to bed equally noisily. She'd reached no conclusions—except that she thoroughly disliked Mr. Atkins. Steve, now—he was different. He'd hogged the limelight, and she resented it, didn't think it fair. But he was awfully nice to Beth, and for that she liked him. She wandered back into the kitchen, fixed herself some breakfast, and took her tray out to the patio.

Might as well make the best of this lonely living. As soon as she finished toast and juice she'd get Hemingway's

The Old Man and the Sea and start her book report for English.

The kitchen door slammed and Tim took the porch steps in a single bound. "All alone?" he asked.

"Nobody's home." She looked at him closely. "Somebody got a haircut," she observed. "Your ears show again."

"Too short?" Tim looked dismayed. "I told the guy to take it easy."

"You got your money's worth." She laughed at his alarm. "It's good, really," she assured him. "Mom and Dad will like it."

"Now I know it's too short." Tim rubbed at his head with the back of his hand as if he were trying to make the hair grow right *now*. He looked awkward, and Linda noticed that it was because he held a tennis ball.

"You playing tennis?" she asked.

Tim looked at the ball, squeezed it a few times, transferred it to his other hand, and repeated the process. "Nope, developing muscles."

"Huh?"

"Building my muscles," he said. "Mostly it's good for baseball, but it helps in football too." He reached down, picked up the remaining slice of toast, and took a bite. "Mom mad at you?"

"Why?"

"Oh, I don't know." Tim took another bite of toast. "Just that when I was going to wake you up this morning she said skip it. And she—her voice sounded sort of frosted. Know what I mean?"

Linda was afraid she did. "I guess they're both mad at

me," she said. "Do you like Mr. Atkins?" she asked abruptly.

"Steve's old man?" Tim shrugged. "Okay, I guess. Looks like a fat toad. He sure laps up the praise. To hear him talk, it's like he's on the field carrying the ball instead of Steve." He shoved the last piece of toast in his mouth and shifted the tennis ball to his right hand.

Squeeze, squeeze, squeeze. Watching was monotonous, yet Linda couldn't seem to stop. Tim was always trying to develop muscles—one set or another.

"Sure glad Dad doesn't eat me up like that guy Atkins does Steve." Tim wiped a few crumbs from his mouth. "I mean, he's got Steve All-Star already. If he doesn't make it his dad's going to throw a fit. I bet that guy'd move mountains to make Steve the champ."

"Maybe."

"No maybe. For sure. The guy's just that way." Tim felt his wrist with his free hand. "Can just about feel them getting stronger," he said. "Seems funny," he mused, "having Dad and Atkins in business together. They're so different. But Dad says that the contract should be his, no matter what. Says this is a big break."

Then the contract *wasn't* lost. Linda felt a little better. *Squeeze, squeeze, squeeze.* The *other* football families—was this tennis-ball routine making them feel wacky too? She giggled at the picture.

"What's so funny? My hair?" Tim's hand went up to his shorn head.

"I was just thinking how funny you football heroes must look—all in line, squeezing tennis balls. You should do it to music, like some of the routines we have in Physical Ed."

"Only Bud and me know about it. I told him last night. Doug was telling me about it. You can even—"

"Doug?" Linda studied her plate so Tim wouldn't see the interest in her telltale eyes. "Doug who?" she prodded.

"The guy who brought me home in the jalopy yesterday. His dad's a coach or something down South. He—" Tim eyed her suspiciously. "What do you mean, 'Doug who?' He says he knows you."

"I'm sure, dear brother, there's more than one Doug at Claremar."

"Okay, okay. Anyway, his dad—"

"How come he goes to school up here?"

Tim shrugged. "Beats me. Something to do with his mom. Clammed up when I asked."

"Maybe that's why he doesn't do anything around school. Because he wishes he were down South."

"I don't know. Anyway, about these muscles—"

"He could have gone to the game last night."

"He works. Four to ten. The jalopy's his boss's. Hope I land a job like that when I get my license. Anyway, these muscles—here, try it. Feel 'em build up." Tim tossed the ball to her and Linda attempted to squeeze it. She couldn't feel anything develop except frustration. She couldn't even manage a good squeeze.

"Hand it back." Tim looked at her scornfully. "Girls are weak."

"He could have gone to the dance. It didn't start till after ten."

"Who could have?" Tim asked.

"Doug."

65

"Doug? Doug who? After all, dear sister, there must be more than—"

Linda felt her face redden. "Stop it, Tim." she demanded.

"Okay." Tim's eyes were teasing. "Only that reminds me, I've got a TL for you."

TL or trade last meant a compliment—only you had to give one before you got it. Linda searched in her mind for a compliment to give Tim.

"Beth thinks you're cute."

"I've heard that."

"Vickie and Mary Lou think I'm lucky to have you for a brother."

"That's fact, not flattery."

"Come on," Linda begged, "tell me. I'll give you a TL free next time."

"It's corny," Tim said. "Really isn't much. Just that Doug said you looked like a princess in blue." He laughed. "Told you it was corny."

Princess in blue. That day in the hall. What else had he said? She felt her face grow hot, saw her brother's eyes widen as he watched her. She could almost hear the wheels in his head spin.

"Princess in blue," he repeated. "Say—that day—I always wondered why—"

"Exercise your muscles." Linda put down her plate and glass and fled for her room.

So Doug had a job. Was that why he had turned her down? No. A job was a legitimate excuse. And he'd been so abrupt. Linda changed her clothes and tidied her room. Maybe he didn't know how to dance. Phooey on that rea-

66

son. He looked as though he'd be a good dancer. She changed the towels in the bathroom and cleaned the fixtures. She wished Mom and Dad would get home soon. She didn't enjoy having them away like this, having them displeased with her. Maybe she could explain a little about last night.

She heard the whir of the mower and knew that Tim was tackling his weekly chore of lawn cutting. Johnny and Jeff came home starving and she fortified them with peanut-butter-and-jelly sandwiches. They gulped down their food, drank huge quantities of milk, and were off again. She straightened up the kitchen, did the dishes. Maybe Mom would notice, and know that this was Linda's way of saying she was sorry. What about Dad? Perhaps if she started her editorial—the one Mr. Benning suggested— on responsibility and straight thinking . . . Dad liked her to write, said she was developing her talent. She went back to her room and took the cover off the typewriter. It was an old one Dad had had in school. But she'd become attached to it, and it was certainly good enough for her two-finger pecking system. As she slipped a piece of paper in, she heard Tim rummaging in the kitchen. In a couple of minutes he stood at her door, a three-decker sandwich in his hand.

"Going up to Bud's," he said.

"Okay."

She heard the front door slam. She was alone again. The paper looked so *blank*. Maybe she could talk it over with Beth a little.

Linda dialed the number. She was expected to stay

home, but maybe Beth could come over. Three rings. *Come on, Beth, be home.* Four . . .

"Hello?" Beth's voice was breathless.

"Hi, it's me. Linda."

"Oh. Hi, Linda. I—"

"I wondered if you could come over." Linda settled herself in the chair and sprawled her legs across one another. "I need your help."

"Golly, Linda, I—I'm expecting a call from Steve. And, well, do you mind if we don't *talk* now?"

Linda said her good-by briefly and hung up the phone. Beth hadn't said anything about coming over—hadn't even *suggested* that she go there. Always on Saturdays, she and Beth— But that was before Steve. She sat with her hand on the phone. There was Mary Lou, or Vickie. But they were second choice, second best. She wanted first choice. She wanted to *be* first choice. The phone rang under her hand and she jumped. She picked up the receiver.

"Hello?"

"Linda?" It was Mom. Her voice was—was still frosty. "We're at your grandparents'. We'll be here awhile; then Dad's stopping at the Atkinses. We may be late, so—"

"Want me to start dinner?"

"Just for you and the boys. Why not have Beth down? We'll be home to change, but we're going out."

No need to tell Mom that Beth wouldn't come. No need to say that she wished Mom and Dad were home so she could *explain*. No need for *anything*. Linda listened to Mom's directions as to what to fix, her instructions that Tim was not to go out.

"About last night," Linda cut in desperately.

"Just remember this, Linda Chapin," her mother's crisp voice said. "You father is a wonderful man."

The phone clicked, went dead, and Linda realized that Mom had hung up—that she didn't want to listen to explanations. Linda turned from the phone and climbed the stairs. Her legs felt wooden, heavy. She looked at the typewriter with its clean sheet of paper. Her editorial? She didn't feel like working on it. She had other problems. Maybe if she listed them? *Them?* Just one. "A is for Atkins," she typed. That summed it up nicely.

CHAPTER 8

SHOW AND TELL

Monday at last! The weekend had been frustrating, depressing. Linda's misunderstanding with her father hadn't been resolved, just ignored. Somehow there hadn't been a right time to talk things out, and now it was as though she'd entered into a sort of truce with her parents. A truce over *what?*

Linda stacked her books on the dining-room table, checking to be sure she had everything. She was walking to school today because Beth planned to go with Steve. She retrieved her lunch from the refrigerator and kissed her parents good-by.

"Want to jog with Bud and me?" Tim asked. "The exercise'll do you good. Develops muscles."

"No, thanks." She had to smile at the picture of herself flanked by the two boys jogging at their uncomfortable pace, and probably squeezing tennis balls to boot. Wouldn't *her* friends be amused!

"We'll walk you to the corner," Johnny said. "We'll tell you our speech."

Monday was "show and tell" for fifth graders, and she'd worked out a sample *Clarion* page in dummy form for the twins yesterday in response to their desperate pleading. "Come along, then," she said.

"Thank you, Linda," Mom said. "I appreciate this. I've run out of heirlooms or inspirations for 'show and tell.'" Mom's smile was warm, and Linda felt, almost, as though she *belonged* again.

"Let's *go*," Jeff urged.

The boys kept up their steady chatter to the end of the block. She stood patiently at the corner while they finished their spiel, then watched them start back for home. They were such nice brothers—bratty and bothersome at times, but she loved them.

The air was nippy. Brown leaves snuggled so close together on the lawns and sidewalks that they formed thick blankets. The trees looked scraggly—like balding men who refused to accept their losing battle and combed their remaining strands into a sparse crown.

Linda walked along briskly, glad she'd worn her bulky knit sweater. The leaves crunched and crackled under her feet. The weekend had been unsatisfactory in so *many* ways. Mom and Dad's "social whirl" had caught her unprepared. It was so unlike them. Beth had stayed glued to her home on the chance that Steve might this, that, or the other. And she'd continued to keep the phone free in case he called. It was most dismaying. But most disturbing was the unresolved misunderstanding with Dad. Why hadn't she managed to talk things out? What was the chasm that kept them from communicating? Was it her fault—or Dad's?

Oh, well, she'd caught up on homework, at any rate, read her history assignment, translated her French, typed up her report on *The Old Man and the Sea*. Big fish ate little fish, bigger fish ate big fish, biggest fish. . . . Had Hemingway meant life was like that? It was an unhappy thought. She hoped Mom wouldn't serve fish for a long time.

The girls were waiting by her locker when she reached school.

"Linda, look," Mary Lou exclaimed, her face flushed with excitement, "look at Beth! Isn't it perf?"

"Our friend's made progress," Vickie remarked.

Linda looked. Beth's eyes sparkled, her cheeks were bright pink, her smile almost shy, and on the hand she held out for Linda's inspection was Steve's class ring. *So Beth was going steady, and she hadn't told her first.* "Golly!" Linda fixed a smile on her face and hoped that her exclamation covered up her hurt.

"I'm so excited. It's so wonderful." Beth's eyes danced. "I almost couldn't wait to get to school and show it."

"Golly," Linda repeated. "I—I'm stunned."

"Me too." Beth sighed the words and grinned. "Beautifully, gloriously stunned. Oh, Linda!" Beth turned her hand this way and that, as though she were feasting her eyes on the cumbersome ring. "Steve said to eat lunch with him, but I couldn't. Not today. I have to tell you all about it. I . . ." Beth was babbling now, her tongue almost tripping on her words. "I . . ." First bell rang and they had to disperse to classes. "At noon, Linda," Beth promised as she raced off down the hall.

Linda clicked her locker shut and walked swiftly to English. What did you say when your best friend went steady? "Golly" was inadequate. Beth expected more. Maybe by lunchtime a suitable congratulatory speech would form. She tried to plan one out as she dodged through the crowded

72

hall to her room. She sideswiped a fellow student and almost lost her books.

"Steady does it," an amused voice told her, and she looked up to see Doug regarding her quizzically. His half smile taunted her and she turned quickly away. She was not in the mood for taunting smiles.

By the time she reached U.S. history, Linda had become stoically calm. The teacher sprung a surprise quiz and Linda filled in the answers swiftly, grateful that she'd at least read the chapter. She glanced across the room at Beth and almost stopped writing. Beth sat nibbling on the end of her pen, looking at her ringed finger, seemingly unaware that a quiz was in progress.

At the period's end Beth waited at the door for Linda. "Don't scold," she said. "Don't nag. It was only a quiz."

Only a fat, irrevocable F. Linda kept silent.

"I—Steve and I came by this morning to tell you. I wanted you to know first," Beth went on. "Only you'd gone."

Linda felt mollified. Beth *had* tried. "Didn't you study at all?" she asked.

"Huh-uh. Phooey on books." Beth shrugged as if she were tossing off her responsibilities. She laughed at Linda's shocked expression. "You look preachy," she said, wrinkling her nose in distaste. "You look so—so—"

"Too too?" Linda asked.

"Too too." Beth held out her hand so she could see the ring. "I guess," she added with a shrug, "you can't understand. You've never felt this way." Her voice sounded smug, superior.

Linda tried to laugh it off. "I understand I'll get a cut if I'm late for Physical Ed." she said. "See you at lunch."

Linda zipped into Physical Ed just as the last bell rang. She changed into her swimsuit, tucked her hair into her cap, and stood under the biting cold of the shower. If Steve were affected like Beth, the results might be disastrous. Poor grades meant no sports. That was one of Claremar's standing rules. What if Mr. Atkins got the idea that Beth interfered with Steve's grades? Would he pressure Steve into breaking up? Linda could hear his voice now. *"Nothing . . . nobody . . ."* She shuddered. Beth better watch her step.

Lunch—biology—and now journalism. Linda plunged into her work. She was back on familiar territory. Lunch hour had produced no "confidences" but a flood of congratulations. It was as though royalty had bequeathed unexpected honor on a commoner. Beth, who formerly had considered "going steady" as a confession of insecurity for both parties, now seemed to regard it as the ultimate in a girl's life. Linda marveled that news traveled so fast, that so many people were twittery. Of course Steve had achieved a hero's role in Friday's game. Linda felt pushed aside, ignored. Now, in journalism, she became a person again. Not too much work on the *Clarion* today, but plenty of publicity releases for the Hi-Jinks.

"Say, Linda," said George, "how about deciding who gets what teacher for our Swat-the-Faculty booth?"

"We'll draw names. That's fairest," Linda said. As she copied the names from the faculty roster onto slips of paper, she felt her spirits soar. The *Clarion* booth was going to be real fun. She piled the tags into a box and watched the varied expressions as her classmates read which teacher effigy they would make.

"Think I'll do right by the Dean of Girls?" George asked as he pocketed his name tag.

Mr. Hall laughed. "Just make us dummies durable," he said. "I've a hunch we're in for rough treatment."

The enthusiasm of the *Clarion* staff seemed almost tangible. And it wasn't just for *their* booth, but for the whole idea of Hi-Jinks—wonderful, wonderful Hi-Jinks. Linda wondered how she'd let things and people get out of proportion. The Hi-Jinks was the important thing. Raise money for the exchange students. Work for what you wanted most. Today had been show and tell for Johnny, Jeff—and Beth. From now on every day would "show-and-tell" day for Linda and the Hi-Jinks. She tackled her publicity release with blissful ecstasy. For the next couple of weeks she'd show 'em. She'd tell 'em!

CHAPTER 9

HI-JINKS

Just as a rose is a rose is a rose is a rose, so a day is a day is a day is a day. Only some roses are extra-beautiful, prize-winning. And some days are like that too.

Linda pulled back the window shade and looked out at Saturday's early dawn. The sky was a pearl-gray shell edged with cotton-candy pink along the horizon. Today was going to be extra-beautiful. Today was Hi-Jinks. It made Linda feel wonderful, just to be sixteen, and a junior, just to be alive. How could she wait until ten o'clock when she reported at the school—or eleven o'clock, when Hi-Jinks officially opened! She turned back to her room. The bed looked inviting. The rest of the family wouldn't awaken for quite a while. Now that she'd checked on the weather maybe she could relax.

She settled back against her pillow and pulled her covers snugly around her. Football games, midterms, the *Clarion*, publicity for Hi-Jinks—what a jumble of activities these past days had been. Beth would be working in the rally commission's dart booth. Maybe they could have lunch together. Or would Beth be eating with Steve? Linda was learning the hard way to mind her own business. Beth's "D" in U.S. history had shocked them both. No report turned in, and she'd flubbed the big exam.

"It's for Claremar too," Beth insisted, when Linda tried to tell her she shouldn't do so many of Steve's papers for him. "Steve's got to keep eligible to play, and he gets so tired from practice." Now that the first marking period was over, he was set for the rest of the season. Maybe now Beth could concentrate more on her own studies. . . .

Linda heard a slight noise and held her breath as she listened. Mom up? No. It was Tim—or Dad—snoring. Both seemed so exhausted these days—Dad with his pages of estimates on the Atkins motel, and Tim with football. Her throat contracted with remembered fear from the day Tim had lain so still on the football field and had been helped to the bench. But he'd gone back in the last quarter of the freshman game, apparently recovered. How could Mom stand it?

She stretched under the covers, her muscles aching slightly from last night's work on the booth. *How many others had creaking joints?* she wondered. If only Hi-Jinks would be successful, if only Swat-the-Faculty would go over big. So much work for one short day—one beautiful, scrumptious, gorgeous day, one happy, happy, happy day . . .

"Hey, Mom says wake up!" Johnny's and Jeff's united yell brought her to her feet. She dressed hurriedly and brushed her hair back into a pony tail.

"Pour the juice and make some toast, will you, dear?" Mom asked when Linda walked into the kitchen.

"Our men will be here in a minute." Mom cubed the cheese and added it to a bowl of beaten eggs. Butter bubbled gently in the frying pan. "I hope today will be just perfect, Linda."

77

"Mmm, me too." Linda said the words almost like a prayer.

The juice was poured, the third batch of toast buttered, when Dad walked in, followed by the three boys. Somehow they reminded her of the wooden duck family she'd pulled along on a string as a little girl.

"All set for the big day?" Dad asked. "You must have ordered the weather, Linda."

"We all did," said Tim.

"Yes, sir," Johnny piped up.

"And how!" echoed Jeff.

"Quack, quack," said Linda, and felt her face get hot as her family turned startled eyes in her direction. She sat down at the table quickly hoping to hide her confusion. "Toast, anyone?"

"She'll be okay tomorrow," Tim assured his father. "She's just flipped temporarily."

She glanced up and caught Mom's amused smile as Mom set the platter of omelet on the table. *Mom knew.* Somehow she and Mom caught each other's thought waves. It was such a *together* feeling. She giggled.

"I know a joke about ducks," Johnny offered. "Something about quackers."

"Aw, you goofed it," Jeff said.

"It's too early for jokes," Tim protested. He turned to Linda. "Bud and I'll get there about lunch," he said.

"We'll remind the kids in the park," Jeff said. "Then we'll come up."

"Since we're working on the PTA dinner, we'll patronize your booth afterward, okay?" Mom's eyes smiled at Linda.

78

"Okay." Linda eyed the clock anxiously as she crumbled a crust of toast. The minute hand was moving toward ten.

"Should bring back memories, Martha," Dad said. "The 'Swat' booth."

"Those teachers from *our* day, Fred?" Mom poured seconds on coffee as she spoke. "Maybe I'll get rid of a few aggressions I've held all these years."

Her parents must have had a lot of fun when they were young, Linda mused. She tried to picture them as teenagers. She fidgeted. She'd be late if Dad didn't hurry.

"She's got ants in her—" Tim started to say.

"Tim." Mom sounded reproving.

Dad pushed back his chair. "I'll drive you up right now," he said. "I'll have thirds on coffee when I get back." He put down his napkin and stood up. "See you at the car, princess."

" 'By, everybody." Linda gave Mom a peck on the cheek. "Wish us luck." She hurried to the car. As she waited for Dad to unlock it the sunshine dimmed momentarily. Linda looked up. It was only a cottony white cloud, but she wished she could reach up and push it aside. No cloud should laze across the sun's rays today.

Later Linda was to remember Hi-Jinks as divided into three parts. She knew when she first got there that only the working crew would be on hand. But even after Hi-Jinks officially opened, the crowds were sparse. In fact, there weren't really any crowds. And no one patronized the "Swat" booth.

"Don't worry so," said George, who'd signed up for an early shift. "Most of the kids aren't even up yet."

79

Linda hoped he was right, but was afraid he wasn't. By two o'clock she *knew* he wasn't. "Scattered crowds," she paraphrased a weather report. Only two tickets were in the "swat" jar—both from one boy, the principal's son, who'd taken delight in "swatting my old man," as he so inelegantly put it.

"Relax," said Sandy, who as *Clarion's* editor-in-chief had first choice on work shifts. "The reason I picked this time is because I knew I wouldn't have much work."

Linda wandered from booth to booth disconsolately. Hi-Jinks was a flop. "Swat" was more so. She bought a hot dog. Maybe she'd go over by the tennis court and relax. No one would be there.

She sat down on the lawn outside the courts' high fence. When she'd consumed the last morsel of bun she stretched out on the grass on her stomach and rested her head on her arm. A bee cruised nearby and buzzed her in its aimless flight. It was a soothing sound, and she closed her eyes and mind to thoughts of the Hi-Jinks and felt as though she were drifting into a sort of neutral nothingness. Drifting . . . drifting . . . And then she was being tugged back into the *now* by an ant or something crawling up and down her arm. She tried to brush it away, but it evaded her hand. She opened her eyes and raised her head—and sat upright. *Doug.* He held a long blade of grass in his hand.

He laughed at her flustered expression. "I didn't know princesses slept with their mouths open," he said.

"I—I—" Linda felt her face flame.

"Your dad—I told him I'd find you," Doug continued. Linda looked, startled, at her watch. She'd slept two hours! She stood up quickly and almost fell because her foot hadn't awakened with the rest of her. Doug steadied her. "I'm okay," she said, brushing aside his arm impatiently, hiding her confusion with brusque words. "I'll get right back." She picked up her purse. "Thanks." She started across the lawn to the walk.

"Linda."

She turned, facing him.

"I have to go back to work now. But tonight—at the dance maybe?" His voice held a pleading note.

Linda turned on her heel, not answering, and started to run toward the carnival. Let one Doug Johnson know what it felt like to be rebuffed, humiliated.

Back at Hi-Jinks, she was amazed at what a difference two short hours had made. The scattered crowds had more than quadrupled. Everywhere there were noisy youngsters, restraining parents. Not many of her colleagues were around yet, except for the ones working.

She saw Beth in the rally commission booth, giving a small girl a pompon for her dart-throwing ability. "Be back as soon as I see my folks!" she called. Too bad she and Beth and Vickie and Mary Lou hadn't synchronized their work hours better. As she hurried on she glimpsed her other two friends at the Spanish-club booth, munching tacos.

"Isn't it perf?" Mary Lou called.

Linda nodded as she opened the door into the cafeteria. Mom was breaking up pieces of lettuce. Dad stood serenely, slicing and buttering French bread. Tim and Bud expertly filched a couple of end crusts and munched on them. They never ever seemed to get enough to eat.

"You're found," Tim mumbled with his mouth full. His glance scanned the room. "Where's Doug?" he asked.

Linda shrugged. "Work," she said briefly. "Did you want me, Dad?"

"We just *missed* you," he said. "Everything's under control here—unless you could manage to get rid of these hunger-hounds for us," he added.

"How's the booth?" Mom called.

"The potential swatters haven't arrived yet," Linda answered, and felt a sort of relief in her own words. That was probably the case.

"Go have fun. We'll see you at supper," Dad ordered. "All of you."

Linda saw Tim reach for another slice of bread as she turned to leave. "Come on," she said. "Give Dad a break."

The two followed her as she made her way past the various booths. But when she stopped at the handcraft table they left her.

"Girls," Bud said with disgust. And she saw that as the boys walked away they were squeezing the tennis balls again.

The rest of the afternoon and evening sped by on wings. Linda caught occasional glimpses of her twin brothers. They were always in a frenzied hurry, it seemed. The Hi-Jinks got more crowded by the minute, and Linda saw, happily, that Swat-the-Faculty had as much of a crowd around it as any other booth. The varsity football team arrived en masse just about the time all the lights went on. Now, Linda decided, the carnival looked like some magic playland. Shouts, laughter, and the steady hum of voices made a cacophony of sound. What a glorious, wonderful Hi-Jinks!

She and Beth could at least have supper together. They stood in the long line against the wall to the "caf" entrance. Linda was glad to lean against the wall. She felt so tired that she wanted support. As they stood there, Steve came up with Bob Brown, and Beth let them in ahead of her. They, in turn, permitted a few of their friends to squeeze in. So now Linda and Beth were separated. Linda took her tray of food and went alone to a different table from the one she and Beth had originally picked. Beth wouldn't want to be bothered with her now. Her shoulders sagged with disappointment.

"Pep up, kid, and move over."

Linda looked up to see Steve, Bob, Beth, and the others crowd in at the table. As they ate and exchanged parries, Linda felt alive, gay, unlike the serious self she usually was. She saw Dad grin at her approvingly. This he *should* like—seeing her in the company of the great Atkins' son. All too soon they were through and had to take up their trays so that the still hungry could find seats.

Back in the milling throngs Linda thought how nice Beth and Steve looked together as they walked down the corridors hand in hand. She walked swiftly to her own booth and relieved the girl on duty.

"Have fun," she told her.

"Having food first," the girl retorted.

Vickie came by to take a few swats at her science teacher. "Want a ride home?" she asked. "I'm on clean-up and I have the car."

"Sure," Linda said. She'd agreed to clean-up too.

Through the throng that crowded the swat-the-faculty booth Linda caught an occasional glimpse of the dance at

Ye Olde Corrall. She saw Steve and Beth, George and his girl, Tim and Angela. Maybe she should have allowed herself some time at it. Maybe Doug . . .

By the time Mom and Dad came by for their swats, followed by Jeff and Johnny, who insisted on theirs, many a stuffed dummy had been laid to rest and the effigies of other, less popular teachers had taken their places. Now Mom could see for herself how popular the booth was. Dad looked relieved when Linda told him she had a ride home.

Almost closing time. The day had been long. Linda was ready.

"Where have you been, Linda?"

She looked up to see Mr. Benning and his wife. "I've been by before," he continued. "But always you weren't here."

Linda smiled at him as he chose his victim. Just as he was ready to take his licks, his arm was jostled by a crowd of boys: the football team. Steve and his friends looked flushed, almost feverish, as they pushed and shoved their way along. Linda saw Mr. Benning's eyes cloud and his lips tighten. He shook his head slightly as he took fresh aim. Linda felt surprise. After all, you expected to get shoved once in a while in a crowd like this.

"It is too bad," he said heavily as he laid down the paddle. He turned and walked off slowly, propelling his wife along as he went. *What was too bad?* Linda wondered.

Now the lights dimmed. The Hi-Jinks was over. In a matter of minutes the carnival area was cleared of customers. Only the work crews remained. As Mr. Hall and Linda stacked up the dummies and took apart the booth the custodian strode by.

"The mess I don't mind," he said angrily, "but beer cans, yes."

"Beer cans?" questioned Mr. Hall.

"Bottles too," the custodian emphasized. "A pile of them." He strode off, muttering, as Mr. Hall looked after him with a puzzled expression.

"Probably little kids," said Linda. "Like the summer at Yosemite when my twin brothers collected all the cans and bottles in the camp grounds and stacked them by our tent. Was Mom ever embarrassed!"

Mr. Hall tugged at the last of the crepe paper without answering. He shoved it and the cardboard into the trash can. Now the booth was completely dismantled. "Let's check these at the cashier's," he said, handing Linda a couple of jars filled with stubs. "Looks like this booth was a winner."

Linda agreed. It did seem that way. Vickie's jars, for example, as she came up to them were full, but not stuffed.

"All set?" asked Vickie. "Ready to leave?"

"Go ahead, Linda," urged Mr. Hall. "I'll be leaving in a couple of minutes myself."

It took effort for Linda just to put one foot in front of the other as she and Vickie crossed the grounds to the sidewalk. "It was fun, but I'm beat," she told Vickie.

"Me too." Vickie smothered a yawn. "And to think I did this all for you."

"Me?"

"Sure. Our next year's exchange student. Isn't that what the money's for?"

Our next year's exchange student. That had sounded good, coming from Vickie. Linda hoped it was true.

"The car's two blocks down," said Vickie. "I couldn't park any nearer. And to think, the Fields picked up Beth and Mary Lou right at the entrance."

Linda and Vickie had almost walked the first block when a car screeched around the corner on two wheels. Steve in his convertible with his buddies!

"Linda, Vickie!" he yelled, and the girls were pelted with water balloons that splatted against the pavement, splashing water on their legs. Before they could protest, the car sped off, swerving to the wrong side of the street, then back into its own lane.

"Ugh, my shoes are—" began Linda, when a grinding crash of metal against metal shattered her thought. The boys. Both girls broke into a run.

CHAPTER 10

EYEWITNESS

As they raced toward the corner Linda felt sick. *Was anyone hurt?* Steve . . . Bob . . . There was always something so brutal when cars collided and crunched against each other like monsters headlocked in the fury of destructive battle.

Doors were opened, porch lights blazed as people hurried to the crash. With a part of her mind Linda noted that the arterial stop had been Steve's to obey. The cross street had none. Had he stopped—or even slowed down?

"They're all okay," Vickie said. "I've even counted them. And no one looks hurt."

Linda saw the boys gathered by the convertible's left rear fender. The expression on Steve's face was one of disbelief, as he ran his hand over his close-cropped hair.

"I've phoned the police," a man was saying. "They're on the way."

Linda looked over at the other car, a jalopy, and an icy finger of fear ran down her spine. *Doug.* She could see him, white-faced, still sitting in the car. A man pulled at the door, trying to open it. Doug seemed too dazed to help.

Now the door was open. "You okay, son?" the man asked. He reached in to help Doug out, and Linda felt her heart pound. *Doug. He was hurt.* But no, he got out slowly, straightened up, and walked to the front of the car.

"The car," he said. Despair laced his voice. "It's my boss's."

"A couple hundred should fix it," the man said. "Boy, you sure smacked him."

The wail of a siren rose above the crowd's noise and Linda saw the flashing red light as the patrol car came to the scene. Someone had lighted a couple of flares to warn approaching motorists. Some of the crowd, satisfied that no one was hurt, began to disperse.

"Only a crumpled fender and smashed tail light," reported Vickie. "Steve's lucky."

Linda nodded. The jalopy had taken the brunt of the crash. A widening pool of water meant that the radiator was damaged, and the fender was buckled at a crazy angle against the left wheel. The one working headlight glared on uselessly, and Linda wished that someone would turn it off.

Vickie moved back to Steve and Bob, and Linda felt herself apart from the others as she watched. Steve's jaws worked rhythmically over a piece of gum, but he stopped chewing long enough to say something to Bob. As the two patrolmen beckoned to Steve and Doug, Linda saw Bob sort of fade into the background. One patrolman was the policeman who'd stopped Steve the night of the rec dance.

Steve looked almost nonchalant as he presented his driver's license. Doug looked grim as he handed over his card. Linda turned away, and her wandering gaze focused, suddenly, on Bob. He'd pulled his jacket from the convertible, and it looked bulky as he carried it over his hands. She heard a *clink*—metal, glass, she didn't know. Only it struck her as odd that a jacket should clink. Bob's glance caught hers, and he seemed to back away.

She looked back toward the policemen. Now Vickie was talking to them. What could *she* say? The girls hadn't seen the accident—but they had seen Steve's driving. . . . Linda's gaze again searched the crowd for Bob. He was at Doug's car now, leaning in, as though he were reading the registration. He straightened up, slipped on his jacket, and rejoined Steve.

Now the crowd had dissolved into a handful of stragglers. Porch lights went off, front doors were closed. Linda wanted to leave. Vickie, she saw, was no longer talking to the police. She went over and touched her friend's arm. "Let's go," she said. "We can't do anything staying."

She saw friendly recognition light Doug's face, then watched it disappear as Steve said "Give me time to tell Beth first, okay?"

"Okay," Vickie agreed for them both.

I should have said I was sorry, let Doug know he wasn't all alone, Linda thought as she and Vickie walked down the block. He'd looked—*forlorn.*

"Accidents make you want to drive carefully," said Vickie as they got in her car. "Want to stop for a hamburger?"

"I just want to get home."

As they drove up to her house Linda decided that perhaps she'd been too abrupt. "Why not come in—and have hot chocolate," she asked.

"Why not?" Vickie turned off the ignition and followed Linda up the walk.

Linda opened the front door and kicked off her shoes

simultaneously. When they walked into the living room she had to giggle. Mom and Dad had their shoes off too, their feet resting on the coffee table. Beat feet must run in the family.

"We'd have gotten home earlier, only we saw an accident," Linda said.

"Auto?" asked Dad. "Anyone hurt?"

"No one hurt," interposed Vickie quickly. "May I take off my shoes too?" she asked as she sank down into the wing chair.

"Why not," Dad said. He stretched back on the davenport. "That Hi-Jinks was a workout."

"But oh, the money we made." Mom patted the davenport as an invitation for Linda to sit down. "We must be way over the goal."

"I told Vickie I'd make hot chocolate," Linda said. "Okay?"

"I'll make it." Mom slipped her feet into a pair of moccasins. "You look more worn out than I feel."

"Food?" Tim lumbered down the stairs. "Did someone say food? I'm starved."

"Where are Johnny and Jeff? In bed?" Linda asked as she followed her mother into the kitchen.

"Reading comics, most likely. They brought home quite a stack from the White Elephant booth."

Linda sat on the stool and watched while Mom got out the milk, chocolate, and even a bag of marshmallows that she must have had hidden. The way Tim and the twins consumed sweets!

By the time Linda carried the tray into the living room,

the twins were downstairs. "We want in on the party, too," Johnny said.

Dad moved his feet from the coffee table to make room for the tray. Linda pushed the table back slightly and sat tailor-fashion on the floor, leaning against Dad's knees. She looked over her shoulder at him. "You're a pretty good dad," she said.

"Those are pretty kind words, princess, and I appreciate them." Dad set down his cup and started gently to massage Linda's shoulders. Linda relaxed, feeling the tiredness almost melt away.

"This beats a hamburger," said Vickie from the depths of the chair. "This is comfort." She popped a cooky in her mouth and took a couple of sips of chocolate.

"Hamburgers, Mom?" questioned Tim hopefully.

"No hamburgers," Mom said firmly. "Nothing more tonight."

Dad took a few swallows of chocolate and then resumed his massage. Linda looked around the room. A quiet, peaceful family scene. A *Saturday Evening Post* cover: the twins in pajamas, the rest of them sipping chocolate with their shoes off. . . . There was comfort in the firmness of Dad's hands. There was protection too. She remembered how safe she'd felt as a little girl when Dad took her to the zoo and the lions roared. He'd hold onto her real tight as she shivered at the sound. . . .

The ring of the phone broke across her reverie. Tim jumped to answer. Mom and Dad sat tense, waiting; it was so late for a phone call. But apparently it was for Tim. His remarks, his ejaculations of surprise . . . In a couple of minutes he returned, eyes excited. "Steve Atkins was in

91

an accident," he reported. "Some crazy driver plowed into him."

"Was he hurt?" Dad sounded alarmed. "The poor kid. His dad—"

"No one was hurt," Linda said. "It's the one we saw."

"How come you didn't tell us?" demanded Tim. "Steve Atkins is big news. I mean, here you sit drinking hot chocolate without saying a word."

"I said we'd seen an accident." Linda defended herself.

"You weren't in the room," Vickie explained.

"Steve wasn't hurt—you're sure of that?" Dad asked.

"Positive," said Vickie. "We—I mean I—even talked to him afterward."

"So many crazy drivers these days. I hope he gets what he deserves," Dad remarked.

"Steve was the crazy driver," Linda said slowly. "Doug drove the other car. Steve ran the arterial—"

"You can't say that, Linda," Vickie interrupted. "We didn't even see the accident."

"But the way he was driving, throwing those water balloons at us, and—"

"A boy throws a few water balloons and you are ready to accuse him?" Dad sounded incredulous.

Linda was on the defensive and she resented it. She shifted her position so she could see her father more easily. "I'm not accusing," she said. "All I said was—"

"Steve's a crazy driver," Tim filled in, "and he ran the arterial."

"You know the other driver?" Dad asked.

"Doug Johnson, a senior, like Steve."

"Why couldn't he have run the arterial?" Dad asked.

"There is none. He had the right of way—" Linda began.

"Maybe I'd better get home," interrupted Vickie. She stood and slipped on her shoes.

Linda jumped to her feet. She opened the front door. "Thanks," she said. "And thanks for bringing me home."

Vickie paused at the open door. "Good night," she said. "The hot chocolate and cookies were just right." She looked at Linda, her glance a puzzling one. "We're lucky to have Steve to play ball," she said. "See you."

Linda closed the door and faced her parents. Dad was frowning. *Now what?* she wondered.

"I can't understand you," Dad said. "Why didn't you say Steve was in the accident when you first came home?"

Linda shrugged. Steve had asked for time to tell about it first. Besides, Dad seemed so different every time the name Atkins came up in conversation.

"And then to accuse him," Dad continued. "Surely the police were called."

"Yes."

"Then, as a favor to all concerned, let's leave the pros and cons of the accident in their hands. And you mind your own business. Forget about your accusations of who did what."

"But Dad, Steve *is* a crazy driver. He did—"

"All I'm asking is that you keep your opinions to yourself," Dad interrrupted. "Do you understand?"

"Because of the contract, Dad? Is that it?" Linda's voice was barely above a whisper.

"That's a factor," Dad agreed, "but more important, even—"

"Nothing is more important than the contract. Nothing,

nothing, nothing." Linda heard her voice rise. "Yes, Mr. Atkins, no, Mr. Atkins, oh, Mr. Atkins." She made her voice sugar-sweet.

"Linda," Mom warned.

Linda shifted her gaze from Dad to Mom. She looked shocked. The twins looked scared. Linda felt shocked and scared. She hadn't meant to sound like that. She looked back at Dad.

"Perhaps you should go to your room," Dad said heavily. "Perhaps there you can learn to be more reasonable."

Linda turned toward the stairs.

"Take your shoes with you." Dad's voice was like a whip.

Linda picked up her shoes and silently walked upstairs. Dismissed, sent to her room. Dad was treating her like a small child. She sat on her bed and found she was trembling. She felt cold—not weather-cold that blankets could fix, but an inner cold. *Why did she and Dad fight?* How could a day that started so beautifully end like this? She felt spent, physically, emotionally, almost too tired to wash her face and brush her teeth as she got ready for bed.

"Be *more* reasonable," Dad had said, but reasonable didn't mean to compromise your principles. Linda picked up her dictionary and flipped through its pages. "Just, fair-minded." That's what she was trying to be. "Rational." She flipped back a couple of pages. "Intelligent, sensible." So? What was Dad trying to get across? Would it be more *sensible* to do and say the Atkins way—such as that first football game? Because of the motel contract? But this wasn't like Dad— not the Dad she knew. If he had seen Steve's wild driving, seen Doug's despair, Steve's confidence, and the policeman who hadn't given Steve a ticket the other time . . .

she turned off her light. Somehow she and Dad weren't getting through to each other. That was it. It couldn't be that Dad was willing to do anything for a contract. She'd have to try harder. She'd have to explain. Tomorrow. Explain . . . explain . . . explain . . . Her thoughts felt as evasive as clouds as she tried to catch them. She was floating in space, drifting, helpless, and Dad's voice came through, familiar, protective: "Good night, princess, good night, darling." She was safe in harbor, anchored by Dad's kiss.

CHAPTER 11

FILE AND FORGET

Last week had been Hi-Jinks. Now, tonight, on a perfectly good football Friday, Linda sat home alone working on the note cards due next week; the first step of her history term paper. Dad had suggested she might like "American Renaissance in Literature" as her topic, and she did. But there was so much material, she had to be selective. So —Mom and Dad were playing bridge next door; the twins had gone to a movie; and Tim, who never believed in letting studies interfere with pleasure, was at the football game. So were Beth, Vickie, and Mary Lou, for that matter. Tonight the Bobcats were playing their first out-of-town game at a nearby school.

Linda leaned back in the chair a moment to stretch out her kinks. She almost had a backache. At least her quotes, paraphrases, sources, and pages on Irving and Poe were duly noted. These cards were a nuisance but a necessity since she wanted a good grade, and good grades she had to have. Nothing, she was determined, would interfere with her chance for France if she could help it. France was the country to which Claremar's American Field Service scholarship winner would go. Final decision would come from New York, but right now she wanted to be one of the school's four finalists. So instead of being at the football

96

game she was home working. It was that important. She broke open another packet of index cards and continued to write.

Now her hand ached. She laid down her pen and flexed her fingers. She let her mind dawdle, and reflected on the busy, catch-up-on-work week. The only leisurely day had been Sunday, the day after Hi-Jinks. The whole family had slept late.

"Let's have breakfast out," Mom had suggested. "After church." The family had agreed with alacrity.

As they had filed into the pew Linda marveled anew at her handsome family. The twins, darling in white shirts and V-neck sweaters; Tim, who could look good even in a dirty sweat shirt, looked even better in his corduroy jacket. Mom sat between Jeff and Johnny, as usual. Linda sat between Dad and Tim. They knelt in prayer and Dad placed his hand over Linda's. It felt warm and protective, and she looked at him, half smiling. Last night's scene hadn't been forgotten by either of them, but it was forgiven by both. The family was together, a unit. Dad's smile was tender, and he nodded his head ever so slightly as if he'd read her thoughts and agreed. Gratefully, she bowed her head.

Breakfast at the Pancake House had been hilarious. Johnny, Jeff, and even Tim had insisted on telling jokes that were moldy with age. She wondered if they hadn't been in existence even when her parents had been kids.

To complete Sunday's perfection they'd gone to the senior Chapins' for dinner. Linda loved her grandparents. She felt sorry for her friends who had no nearby relatives to visit, who had no one to talk of the "good old days."

They'd sat in the living room watching Grandpa's first

fire of the season crackle away on the hearth as the grown-ups drank their after-dinner coffee and Grandpa quizzed her brothers and her on their schoolwork. Something Jeff said started Grandpa reminiscing, and soon he was telling Linda's favorite—his "snake" story.

Grandpa had been Jeff and Johnny's age then. "We'd collect 'em in sacks on the edge of town," Grandpa said. "And we'd turn 'em loose on Main Street, and what screeches and hollers the ladies would make when they saw a snake." He chuckled. "Saturday morning was always the best time. The place was busy with shoppers."

"What made you stop?" Tim asked. "Run out of snakes? Or did you just get too old for that kind of stuff?"

Grandpa's face sobered. "We grew up," he said. "All of a sudden on a Saturday morning. It's a time I don't like to remember."

"Why?" prodded Jeff.

"A skittish mare," Grandpa said slowly. "She took fright at a snake and bolted."

"Was anyone hurt?" Johnny asked.

"The mare," Grandpa said. "She caught her leg in a hole and broke it. They shot her."

"Wow!" said Tim.

Linda shuddered. *Poor little mare!*

"We paid for her," Grandpa continued. "It took us a long time, but we paid for her. Nobody was too anxious to hire young kids—especially us. But we finally made it." He studied the fire. "We grew up that Saturday, I guess. We learned what responsibility meant. We learned to use reason."

"But that didn't bring back the mare," Johnny said.

"No." Grandpa sighed. "No, it didn't bring back the mare."

Now—now Linda realized that she'd been staring at a page in her book without seeing it. Somehow it seemed that there was a connection between Grandpa's story and the responsibility Mr. Benning talked about—a similarity, even, between snakes and mares and balloons and cars.

It was funny about Steve and Doug and the accident. It was as though it had never happened. She had seen no mention of it in the paper, and when she'd tried to tell Beth about it Beth had said "Let's forget it, okay?" and so she had. But she wondered if Steve or Doug had been given a citation. And she wondered if the police had fixed the blame. And she wondered if her history teacher ever *really* checked over these cards. "Mark Van Doren, *Nathaniel Hawthorne*," she wrote.

It felt good to stop writing when the twins came home from the show. They vied with each other to relate the exciting parts. She was reluctant to hustle them off to bed.

"Hey, Linda," Jeff called down, "we forgot! Who won the game?"

"I don't know."

"Can't you call someone?" Johnny asked. "It must be over."

"Tim isn't home yet," Linda said. "Maybe no one else is."

"Wake us when you find out," Jeff demanded. "Or make Tim wake us."

"Okay."

"Promise?" asked Johnny.

"Promise." Linda settled back in her chair to work again. She heard the twins shuffling around upstairs as they got ready for bed. She was tired enough to go to bed herself and she was certainly getting sleepy. The loud blare of horns took her to the window. She peeked around the drapes.

"He's here!" Jeff yelled. "Tim's here."

He was. And with him—in two other cars . . . Linda let the drapes fall and hurried to the door. As she opened it she heard Jeff and Johnny tear down the stairs in their excitement. "We won, we won!" they cheered.

"We won," Tim echoed. "I brought company to celebrate."

Linda felt her grin stretch as Beth, Mary Lou, and Vickie walked in. They were followed by Steve, Bob Brown, and a couple of other players.

"Want to guess who won?" asked Steve.

"We did," Linda said.

"Steve did," Beth corrected. "The last minute too. The score was eighteen to fourteen up to then."

"I was simply pet!" exclaimed Mary Lou.

Linda saw Bob look at Mary Lou, puzzled. "Petrified," she filled in.

"Want to celebrate?" Beth asked. "Want to go to a drive-in?"

"Stay here," Jeff and Johnny said in unison. "Linda'll make you cocoa. Besides, she can't leave us alone."

"Tim's here," Linda corrected. "But—there's enough milk and stuff, and—"

"Let's." Steve turned to Beth. "Okay, woman?"

"Call next door, Tim," Linda commanded. "Tell Mom and Dad we have company."

"Hey, look—music." Steve switched on the record player. "I'm in the mood," he said. "I might even dig up enough energy to dance."

Johnny and Jeff were catapulted into action by Steve's words and started to push furniture against the wall.

"Well trained," Bob said. "Let's dance." He pulled Linda toward him. "The way you've got your brothers working, you must do this often."

Linda chuckled. Actually, she hadn't even been out on a date since her fiasco with George.

By the time Mom and Dad arrived on the scene the four couples were dancing in the living room and hall with the twins seated on the stairs as avid observers, and Tim playing sitter to the record player.

The couples paused in their dancing while Linda made the introductions. Dad knew Claremar's football players so well, all Linda had to do was remember their numbers; Dad filled in the rest. Steve held out his hand to Dad. "Hope you don't mind us barging in like this, sir." He turned to Linda. "Dad says your father's the best construction man he knows."

Linda watched her father beam. *Chalk up a point for Steve,* she thought. He'd made another win, although with Dad he'd already won.

"We told them Linda'd make cocoa," Jeff prompted from the stairs. "That's why they're staying."

"I'll make it," Mom said.

"And I'll help," Dad added. "Now you boys get to bed."

"Aw, Dad," Johnny protested, "the party's just getting going."

"To bed," Dad insisted. "Your time for parties will come. Tonight is Linda's."

Linda felt herself blush. Had Dad sounded *grateful* because the kids had stopped by? Actually, she was grateful too. It had been a big bore, staying home alone. This was unexpected fun. As the twins plodded upstairs and Dad went into the kitchen the others resumed their dancing. Only Bob stood waiting.

"How come you didn't go to our game?" he asked as they joined the other dancers.

"Homework," Linda said briefly. "My conscience too."

"I've heard about it," Bob said. "That's one reason—"

"Heard about what?" Linda asked.

"Your conscience. It's pretty big, I hear. It's boss."

"You heard about my conscience? Where?"

"Beth, Vickie."

"Doesn't everyone have a conscience? Don't you?"

"I let mine know who's boss."

"But I don't?"

"You're saying that, not me. I think you're a pretty good kid. I mean, you know the score, know which side your bread's buttered on."

"I do?"

"Sure. Like you see something you don't like and it's none of your business, you forget it. Right?"

Linda listened. What was Bob getting at?

"Right?" he repeated.

"I—I guess so."

"It's the way I have you figured." Bob smiled down at her. "I figure you for a good dancer too."

"Right," Linda said with impudence. She felt his arm tighten as if he were giving her an approving hug. It was fun dancing with Bob. He was big, almost cumbersome, like a friendly, burly bear.

Tim shut off the record player when Dad called them to the kitchen. They crowded out for the impromptu feast; Mom had done herself proud.

"Perf!" Mary Lou exclaimed as she buttered a biscuit.

"They rate a cheer, Beth, give them one," urged Steve.

"Absolutely," agreed Vickie.

"Okay." Beth stepped onto a kitchen chair. "All together now, a six for Ma and Pa Chapin."

"Fill up your plates," Dad ordered as the last "rah" echoed through the kitchen, "and here are some trays." He turned to Mom. "Ready?" he asked. "We'll be upstairs, princess."

"I agree with Dad," Steve said. "You're the greatest. You too, Mrs. Chapin."

"Thank you, and good night, everyone."

As Dad and Mom left the kitchen Linda found that she had to agree with Mr. Atkins and Steve on one thing. Dad —and Mom—were the greatest.

"Okay if we eat in the living room?" Bob looked from his well-heaped plate to Linda. "I'm beat."

"Fine."

Steve took the easy chair and Beth perched on its arm. Now the group had divided into two parts, with the boys settling down to the serious business of eating and the girls recounting the thrills of the game.

Tim stood up. "I'm for bed," he announced, covering

a loud yawn. "If you want more music, you play for yourselves."

Vickie glanced at her watch. "Oh, no!" she said in a shocked voice. "It's way past midnight. I hate to be a party pooper, but my parents . . ." She picked up her tray and carried it to the kitchen. Mary Lou followed suit. The party was breaking up.

But Steve, relaxed, seemed reluctant to move. "Your friends," he said in mock disgust.

"Sorry." Beth leaned over and kissed him on the forehead. It was such a tender, familiar gesture that Linda looked away quickly, as though she'd been caught invading someone's privacy.

"Guess we better shove off, boss," Bob said. "I'll take your tray. Linda, you take Beth's." He reached down and pulled Linda to her feet.

The parade of the wooden soldiers, Linda thought as she followed Bob into the kitchen, passing the other four on the way. She set the trays on the top of the stove and turned to leave. Bob blocked her way.

"Look," he said, "one thing more I got to know. That Johnson."

"Johnson?"

"I saw his car around here a while back."

"*Doug* Johnson? You mean when he drove Tim home?"

"That's all I wanted to know." Bob's face wore a satisfied look.

"What about Johnson?"

"Nothing. I figured it was like that, anyway." Bob's smile grew to his eyes. "Look," he said, "if I fix it with Steve, how's about doubling tomorrow?"

"Doubling?"

"With Steve and Beth. A show maybe?"

"Come on, Bob, let's go!" called Steve.

"I'll phone you," Bob said as he followed Linda from the kitchen.

Linda stood in the doorway, watching them move noisily down the walk to the cars. Bob hit Steve on the back. "You were all wrong, boss," he said. "No worries at all."

Steve threw a hasty glance over his shoulder. "Shut up, stupid." He gave Bob a shove.

As they drove away, Bob turned and waved. Linda closed the door gently. The kitchen was a mess, but she didn't mind. The evening had been worth it. Somehow it was like having your cake and eating it too. And she had a date with Bob—well, an *almost* date. And if they enjoyed each other's company, maybe she'd have a date to the Grid Classic. Bob was fun tonight, even if he did say peculiar things at times. Her conscience was something others talked about? Beth and Vickie? Why? What was she supposed to forget? Whatever it was, she had apparently filed and forgotten it.

CHAPTER 12

THE CLINK

Linda whipped through her Saturday-morning chores with all the energy of a dynamo. To think that a simple thing like a potential date could give her so much pep, so much drive! *I've been date hungry,* she told her reflection as she polished her mirror. *Starved,* she corrected. She'd missed those comfortable, unexciting dates with good old George more than she liked to admit—they were still friends at school, but he never dropped in casually as he used to —*Thanks to the Fall Frolic—and Doug.*

By lunchtime her chores were finished. She watched Tim put aside his tennis ball reluctantly as he sat at the table. Every time she saw Tim "exercising his muscles" it reminded her of Doug. But she didn't want to think about Doug. She wanted to think about Bob and the fact that maybe tonight she'd be going out. She wanted to say something to Mom and Dad about the date, but she was afraid —afraid it might fall through and then she'd be embarrassed.

"How late did they stay last night?" Jeff asked between bites of sandwich.

"A little after midnight, I guess," Linda told him.

"You looked pretty, kind of. Last night, I mean," Johnny said.

"My, but don't we look happy?" Dad commented. "You're looking as pleased as a Cheshire cat, Linda."

"Last night, I guess," Linda confessed. "You were both so super. My favorite parents."

"Your only parents, goofy," said Jeff.

Linda opened her mouth to protest, then closed it. No use getting in an argument with a brother and spoiling the day.

"We know what you mean," Mom said gently. "And you're our favorite daughter."

"Silly talk," Jeff mumbled into his milk glass. "Women."

The phone rang just as Linda sat down to resume work on her index cards. She made a wild dash for it, but Johnny beat her to it. "It's for you, sis," he said. "A boy."

Linda bit her lip in annoyance as she picked up the receiver. He didn't have to sound as though it were a miracle if a boy called her—even if it was. She kept her voice casual, unconcerned, as she said hello. Bob! Could she go to the show? She relayed the question to Mom and Dad. Certainly. As she placed the receiver gently in its cradle she tried to keep her grin normal size.

"We're doubling with Steve and Beth," she told her parents.

"Great," Dad said. "Good kids. The best." He looked as though he were having as much trouble with a grin as she was.

By date time Linda felt as though she were a nervous wreck. She wondered if she'd break out in a rash or something. She'd changed outfits four times, finally deciding on the powder-blue bulky knit sweater and matching skirt. Her hair was squeaky-clean, and had curled just right.

"Have a good time, princess," said Dad as the doorbell rang. His eyes were warm with approval. Linda felt a quick stab of remembering. "Princess in blue," Doug had called her.

"Want to come here afterward for something to eat?" asked Mom.

Linda shook her head. No use running the free-food angle into the ground.

Bob held the car door open for her. "Nice," he commented as he slid in beside her, and she knew he was pleased with her appearance.

The show was fun, just plain fun. Linda caught the surprised looks on the faces of fellow Claremar students as she and Beth preceded the boys down the aisle. It didn't hurt one's prestige a bit to be seen with a football player. *Status seeker*, she scolded. But she liked it, liked the attention she was getting. George—it had never been this way with George.

Bob rested his arm against the back of her seat, and for a while, Linda hunched slightly forward, tense and uncomfortable. But soon she leaned back and gave herself up to the enjoyment of the movie. Bob's arm felt heavy against her shoulder. Big bear Bob with big bear arms. *All the better to hug you with, my dear*. No. That was the wolf. *Who's been eating my porridge?* Linda giggled.

"What's funny?" Bob whispered. "I didn't get that."

"I was wondering if you like porridge." Linda spoke without thinking.

"Porridge? Do I like porridge?" Bob spoke out loud. "You mean mush?"

Linda felt her face redden. "Shhh," she hissed.

"I do," Bob continued. "With butter and brown sugar and cream. I— How come you asked me that?"

"Shhh," Linda hissed again. "No reason. Watch the movie." She felt Bob's puzzled glance before he looked back at the screen. Linda felt like sliding down in her seat. Why did she always have to goof things up with silly thoughts? She looked over at Beth and caught her amused, sympathetic smile. Beth probably had read her thoughts. It was so very, very good, doubling with Beth. She was such a wonderful best friend. Since Steve, Beth hadn't had as much time just to chum and chat. But now . . .

Later, when they were all squeezed into a booth at the Hamburger Basket, Linda was grateful that she'd told Mom they wouldn't be home for eats. This was living. People stopped by their booth en route to booths of their own or on their way home, and conversation flowed fast and heavy. Linda was fully aware that Steve, Bob, and Beth were the attractions, that she was included only because she was with them, but for once the cat who got her tongue on most occasions had now miraculously taken off for parts unknown, and she was as glib and amusing as the others. She poured a pool of catsup onto her plate and dunked each French fry between bites, savoring the taste and atmosphere. Beth winked at her. A feeling of well-being enveloped her with the steady, penetrating warmth of an electric blanket. Could she—if she went to France this summer as an exchange student—convey this bit of Americana to the family with whom she would live? If only she could! She sighed happily and leaned back in the booth.

"Hey, what's the matter?" Bob asked. "You unhappy?"

Linda shook her head. "Just thinking, *mon ami*," she said.

"No fair." Bob put his hand over hers. "Brains are for the birds."

That was a switch. Up to tonight Linda had regarded the phrase "bird brains" as derogatory—but in a different sense. She wondered about her hand. Should she leave it on the table? It felt uncomfortable. It felt as though it were going to twitch. This was ridiculous, to sit in a booth with a boy and worry about your *hand*—but she couldn't ever remember in any of the etiquette books she'd read about how to retrieve a hand. She willed it to be still, and looked over at Beth. Maybe she . . .

". . . fixing his wagon," she overheard Steve say. He nodded his head and Linda followed Beth's gaze to the counter. Doug!

Instinctively she jerked her hand free from under Bob's. As she moved, her sleeve brushed against her knife and spoon and they clattered nosily to the floor. Red-faced, she bent down to pick them up, and clunked her head sharply against Bob's as he bent to her rescue. They both sat up quickly, spoon and knife still on the floor.

"I don't need them. Leave them," Linda murmured, miserable with embarrassment.

Steve and Beth were laughing at them. "I guess you might say," Steve put in dryly, "you have a hardheaded date, Bob."

"I guess I might." Bob rubbed his forehead ruefully. "Hurt?" he asked.

Linda shook her head. "Embarrassed," she said truthfully. She picked up her hamburger and bit into it cautiously, afraid, suddenly, that she might pull another boner—like knocking over the catsup bottle, or tipping the glass of Coke. Darn that Doug Johnson, he'd embarrassed her again. *Be honest, Linda,* she told herself, *he didn't make you jerk your hand.* Furthermore, what earthly difference did it make to him or her if he should see Bob hold her hand?

Conversation resumed its flow and Linda stole a glance at the counter. Gone? No. There he was, over at the cash register. The woman with him. His mother? She must have been quite pretty at one time. Now she seemed timid, unsure of herself. It was a look Linda never associated with adults. Doug caught her glance briefly. She thought for a moment that he was going to smile, but he turned away. As they left, Linda wondered how a *back* could show such defeat. What was it about Doug that seemed so different? He looked thinner than she remembered. Was that it? Or was it the sag to his shoulders? She turned back to her table and saw Steve regarding her gravely. There was an expression in his eyes she couldn't read. She dipped a French fry into the catsup. It was cold, flat, tasteless. . . .

Linda settled back in the booth and watched Bob consume his hamburger and milk in big, lusty mouthfuls. She had to shake this silly mood she was in. Why should the sight of Doug depress her? What was he in her young life? And, face it, she was no mind reader. How could she expect to "read" Steve's eyes? Bob looked around the table as though he were still hungry.

"Finish my fries?" she asked.

As he ate them she felt amusement replace her depression. Bob—like Tim—apparently consumed large quantities of food, and was still "always hungry." Beth and Steve were in an animated discussion, and Linda listened in.

"Think she'll make grid queen?" Steve asked her. "She'll have the team behind her."

"I'm just a junior," Beth protested. "Queens are usually seniors."

"Sure, but with us . . ."

"Oh, Beth, how perf!" Linda exclaimed.

Beth laughed. "You sound like Mary Lou," then she sobered. "It's—scary, sort of."

"With us rooting for you—the whole team"—Steve's laughing eyes included Linda—"and with the press here—" His voice got confidential. "Give the girl a break, okay?"

"Oh, Beth," Linda repeated. To have Beth grid queen —her best friend—Mary Lou's expression was the only one that fitted. "It *is* perf," she emphasized.

"Agreed." Steve stood up and reached out his hand to help Beth to her feet. "Come on, Bob, let's shove off."

In the car Linda wished fervently that Steve weren't such a fresh-air fan. A convertible in November with the top down was just plain cold. She stretched out her legs until her toes fitted under the front seat. As she nudged her feet more firmly under, she heard a clink.

"Hey, take it easy," Bob said. "Our brew."

"Brew?"

"Beer. You'll break the bottles."

Linda withdrew her feet sharply. Beer? That was against training. Against— "What if you're caught?" she asked.

"Haven't been yet." Bob gave her an elaborate wink.

"Drop it," Steve demanded sharply.

"She's hip, boss," Bob protested. "Right, Linda?"

Hip? Maybe. But hip for what? Linda shrugged. "Guess so," she agreed.

As they drove up to her house Steve braked the car. Bob opened the door and helped her out.

"I'll take Beth home, then pick you up," Steve said. "Okay?" Bob looked at Linda.

"Fine." She led the way into the house. "I'm home!" she called.

"I'm in the kitchen!" Tim's voice boomed out. "Come on in."

Tim sat at the kitchen table, legs stretched out, apple pie and milk before him. "A growing boy," he explained to Bob. "Join me?"

"We just—" Linda began.

"Sure will," Bob cut in.

Linda cut a slab of pie and poured some milk. "Okay, eat up," she commanded. She perched on the kitchen stool and watched them stow away the food. Now the talk was all on football. Linda couldn't refrain from making occasional comments.

"Say, your sister knows what she's talking about," Bob said. There was admiration in his voice.

"She should. She's grown up on it. Dad's a real football fan. Played in Claremar. Second string, though."

"Some girls still wouldn't understand, like—"

"Listen to that guy lean on his horn," Tim interrupted. "He's going to wake up the neighborhood."

"Oh my gosh. Steve." Bob crumpled his napkin and tossed it to the table as he stood up. "Better get going."

Linda opened the front door for him.

"You're a good kid," he said. He patted her on the shoulder. "I'll be seeing you."

Steve's car took off with a screech of tires. Linda shut the door and turned to see Tim standing behind her. "I'm hitting the sack," he said. "I'm beat."

Linda didn't bother to ask if he'd stacked the dishes or put the food away. That would be expecting too much. Maybe if Tim had been a sister— But there wasn't too much to clean up. She rinsed and stacked the dishes and rinsed the empty milk bottles. They clinked pleasantly as she placed them outside for the milkman to pick up. *Clink-clank, like our heads*, she thought. No, that was more of a *thump*. Like the "brew?" As Linda walked to her room she felt as though something—a very *important* something —was eluding her. Bob's sudden attention. It was fun, but why? Why her, of all people? There were lots of Claremar girls much cuter. Because of Beth and Steve? Was it Beth who was pushing this "foursome?" Bob made such strange remarks at times. *Clink*. Her watch fell over on the glass top of her vanity. What was there about a *clink* that should *click?* She snuggled under her covers and willed sleep to come as she wondered.

CHAPTER 13

GIRL'S CHOICE

Linda the lucky—that's who she was, Linda the very, very lucky. It was as though she had miraculously come into possession of a magic charm. It was like being part of a dreamy dream, or floating on pink cloud nine, the way things were working so beautifully.

Beth, officially launched as grid queen candidate; Linda officially appointed her campaign manager; being labeled "Bob's girl" because of the date, the Hamburger Basket, and Bob's walking her to class a couple of times; Mr. Marsh complimenting her on her editorial—the same one Mr. Benning thought "weak"—these were just a few of the reasons she was so lucky. Best of all was having so much in common with Beth again, and the news item Mom clipped from Wednesday's *Herald*. It read:

> *Claremar High School has named four finalists in the American Field Service program. Those whose applications are now sent back to New York are Peter Boudet, Linda Chapin, Sylvia Paley, and Robert Sheldon. One of them will be chosen to live abroad with a family in France for the summer.*

There was more to the story—details of the requirements, and things like that. Mom underlined "Linda Chapin" in red, and it was already in the family scrapbook that Mom kept on family activities or achievements. Dad had bought an extra copy of the paper so he could carry the story in his wallet.

The phone had worked overtime Wednesday evening as Beth, Vickie, Mary Lou, and others called to congratulate her. She made a point of telling them that she was one of four, and only her activities gave her a slight edge . . . maybe. When Bob phoned, he didn't even mention her good fortune, and she'd felt a little hurt until she realized that he never read anything but the sports page. No matter. She couldn't complain. He'd asked her to the Grid Classic, and she'd accepted. Maybe their telephone conversations were dull, but the dance wouldn't be.

One call had surprised her. "A boy," said Jeff as he laid down the receiver.

"Linda? Doug Johnson. I just wanted to say I think it's great, but I'm not surprised. You'll win for sure. You've got what it takes. And tell your Dad he'd better learn to say 'princess' in French. Okay?"

"Doug. Why I—"

"Good-by, Linda." She heard the phone click as the receiver was replaced. She looked at the receiver she still held in her hand. Doug had phoned. How strange! She replaced her receiver. Strange—and somehow special. The only times she saw Doug lately were when he was either going in or out of the dean's or principal's office. And he had such a harassed, strained look about him. They never acknowledged each other in the hall. He never smiled. Odd, that he should call.

And so Wednesday slipped into Thursday, into Friday,

and she continued to float on pink cloud nine until she crash landed with a thud at precisely 9:44 Pacific Standard Time on Saturday morning. The family was enjoying a leisurely breakfast of blueberry pancakes and maple syrup. The twins had stashed their football helmets on the sink and were claiming squatters' rights to the cakes almost as fast as they came off the griddle. Dad had a late-morning golf date with Mr. Atkins, and as soon as Mom and Linda straightened up they were going to track down THE dress for the Grid Classic.

"Hey, your friend got any more new ideas for us, Tim?" Jeff speared a couple of hotcakes onto his plate. "Like squeezing tennis balls?"

"He's a phony and a fake." Tims' voice was harsh with scorn. "He's one for the books."

"We're talking about Doug Johnson," Johnny explained. "I guess you didn't know that."

"He's a phony and a fake," Tim repeated.

"Glad you're not my friend." Linda's words brought a flush of anger to Tim's face.

"And the same to you." Tim's voice dripped with scorn. "I suppose you think I should be buddies with a guy who's out to wreck the school, who's a double-crossing louse, who—"

"Hold it, Tim," Dad interrupted. "Those are harsh accusations. Better not say things like that about anybody unless you can back up your statements."

"I can. Everybody in school can."

"I can't," Linda said. "And we go to the same school."

"You?" Tim snorted. "You can't do anything but write for that dumb *Clarion* or campaign for your dumb friend.

You couldn't back anything because you don't know anything."

"I—I—" Linda jumped up from the table so quickly that she knocked over her glass of juice. "You take that back, Tim Chapin. You—"

"Children." Mom's voice was razor-sharp. "Stop, this instant."

"Yes," said Dad. "Linda, just be seated while Tim starts explaining."

Tim glared at his sister. "I'll tell you," he said. "Remember the accident Hi-Jinks night? Doug and Steve, they were the ones in it."

"We're aware of that." Dad held out his cup for more coffee. "Go on, Tim."

"Doug's saying Steve's to blame."

"And Steve says it's Doug's fault?" Dad shook his head. "Tim, surely you know—"

"Wait, Dad. I'm not through. Doug says more than that. He says Steve was high—on beer. Everybody knows how phony that is. Steve's trying for All-Star. Besides—" Tim's voice dropped to a conversational hiss—"get this. They found two six-packs in Doug's car."

"Six-packs?" Linda's throat became parched.

"Beer. I'm not talking about candy bars."

"What do the police say?" Dad asked calmly.

"They're on Steve's side."

"Police don't 'take sides,'" Mom interrupted.

"That's not what I mean, Mom. What happened is Doug's trying to say Steve had the beer, and he never had any. For a while he even tried to blame his boss. Said the beer must have been his."

As Tim talked, Linda wished desparately that there was a way to erase words.

"You know what this would mean to our team if Doug pinned the blame on Steve, don't you?" Tim paused dramatically. "So Doug the louse will get his, I hear. He's being suspended, or maybe expelled. And Steve's dad is suing."

"Bottles or cans?" Linda's voice sounded unnatural to her ears.

"Bottles or cans?" Tim sounded surprised. "Bottles, cans, cans, bottles. What's the diff? A guy can get high either way." He looked at Linda, shrugged, and added, "Bottles. Imports."

"Well," said Dad. "Well. A smear campaign is dirty playing. Good thing Steve has a father who knows the score." He looked at Linda. "And you were blaming Steve?"

Linda bit her lower lip to keep her mouth steady as she nodded. *Bottles clink*. Milk bottles. Beer bottles. Imports. The night of the show, *in Steve's car* bottles had clinked. Blame Steve? It suddenly became very important to sort thoughts out thoroughly, and alone. She forced her voice to sound natural. "Mom, I think I'll make my bed now," she said.

"A good idea," Mom agreed.

Linda's legs felt shaky, numb, as she walked from the room. She was chilled. She shut the door to her bedroom and sank on the bed. Her glorious world had collapsed in such a few moments and over such a few words. Now she had a problem—a big one, because the facts were there, like puzzle pieces. She was afraid to put them together.

Once the facts were sorted, what then? Bob and the *clink* she had heard when he carried his jacket over to Doug's car. If Steve—and Bob—and the others—had been drinking and had tried to blame Doug, what of Claremar's chances for the championship? What of Steve's chance for All-Star? What about Beth? What about Dad and Mr. Atkins? How many people would she hurt if facts went one way? Would Doug be the *only* one if she just did nothing? Did wrongs ever make a right? And exactly what was it she could do?

She hung up her pajamas and made her bed, wishing she could smooth out problems as easily as one could smooth a bedspread. She folded her sweater and pulled out the drawer to put it away. What a mess! She dumped the drawer's contents onto her bed. She'd put her sweaters in their bags and stack them in neat piles—as she would try to do with her thoughts. And the ones she didn't want, she'd stack underneath. Like her thoughts? Maybe she was jumping to conclusions, wrong conclusions. Did a *clink* prove anything? How could a *clink* prove Steve guilty?

Because Bob was a bribe. Linda's face burned at the thought. His attentions, the date for the Grid Classic, were terms of a contract that Bob assumed she'd accepted. "Like you see something you don't like and it's none of your business, you forget it. Right?" He'd said that the night the kids had dropped by after the game. Football and the championship and Steve's being All-Star were all-important to Bob. *And to how many others?* she wondered.

Beth! She'd forgotten about Beth. It would be hard to tell Beth of Steve's cheating and the *clink*. Maybe she shouldn't put off. Maybe she should go to Beth right now. She would have to explain that Bob was a bribe, but Beth would share her humiliation with her.

She picked up the dresser drawer and slid it into place. Beth could suggest that Steve apologize or something. After all, they'd played lots of games since the accident. Maybe they could finish the season even if they had broken training.

"Almost through, Linda?" Mom's voice was so cheerful that Linda almost felt as though she belonged to a different world. "Dance dresses aren't the easiest to find," Mom continued.

She wouldn't be going to the Grid Classic because Bob wouldn't want to take her. How could she explain that to Mom? Better see Beth first. Better see Beth right now, if Mom wouldn't mind.

Mom looked up as Linda came into the bedroom. "You're wearing that?" she exclaimed.

"Mom." Linda hesitated, then went on in a rush. "Please, may I go to Beth's first? Right now?"

"Phoning won't do?"

Linda shook her head. "And it's terribly important, Mom."

"Hurry, then."

As Linda ran down the stairs a car honked, and she almost collided with Dad at the front door.

"Steady there, princess," Dad said. "If you shake me up too much, I won't give Mr. Atkins a very good game."

Shake him up too much? If he only knew! But first she had to see Beth.

As Dad got in the car Mr. Atkins leaned out the window. "Want a lift?" he called.

"No, thanks." Mr. Atkins looked so sure of everything. Even her?

CHAPTER 14

QUEEN'S PAWN

Linda's pace was almost a run as she hurried to Beth's. Now that she'd decided to share the problem with her friend, she was in a rush to get there. Brown leaves crunched and she remembered how, as a little girl, she pretended that they were crisp cereals that crackled and popped in giant breakfast bowls. Now crunched leaves meant Thanksgiving and the football game. People already referred to the team as "Claremar Champs." Somehow it seemed football was more important to the town than Thanksgiving. Claremar Champs. Was she about to become the Claremar chump?

"Beth's cleaning her room," Mrs. Fields told Linda. "Go on up. She'll welcome the diversion."

Linda could hear the hum of the vacuum as she walked down the hall. She paused momentarily before she rapped. *If only things would come out right!* She knocked again, louder, and heard the motor switched off.

"A minute!" Beth called, and Linda could hear furniture scrape across the floor. Then the door opened.

"Hi." Beth's face broke into a grin. "You're finished shopping already? What's it like? Come on, climb *over*. Can I see it?"

Linda stepped over the shoe rack and edged between the

vanity bench and record player as Beth closed the door. "I—I haven't gone yet," she said. Her mouth felt dry. She tried to swallow. "I had to see you first. It's about Bob."

"Bob? He's hurt? Was Steve with him?"

"No," Linda said quickly. "Nothing like that. It's about Bob and me, because now I know."

"You know?" Beth looked puzzled. "What do you mean, you 'know?'"

"Bob's a bribe." Linda said the words bluntly, then went on in a rush. "Bob's my hush money. So I won't talk. Because of the accident. Because of Steve." Linda couldn't bear to look at Beth—she knew the pain she must be causing her. But she couldn't stop talking, either. Her words spilled over each other like water released from a dam. She told about Tim's words at breakfast, about Vickie, about the *clink* as Bob carried the beer to Doug's car. Finally she turned her gaze on Beth, but Beth had moved over toward the window and was looking out, her face unfathomable. *I'm hurting her. My best friend. I had to be the one.* Her words faltered. "I'm sorry." Linda's voice was a whisper. "I—I just wish . . ."

"Bob didn't call you?" Beth asked. "Bob doesn't know you know?"

"I came here right away."

"Then there's no problem," declared Beth. "And even if Bob does know you know, the situation is still *status quo*. You'll go to the dance with him."

"But when I *tell*, Beth? When I *tell*?"

"When you tell *what*?" Beth's voice was cold. "What do you mean, *tell*?"

124

"Weren't you listening? About the accident. About the beer. About Steve and Doug."

"You plan to tell that? To whom?"

"Mr. Marsh or the police, I guess. That's why I came here. So you could help me."

"You want me to help you ruin Steve?"

"Not ruin Steve, Beth. You're not understanding. Right now Doug's being blamed for something Steve did. He's —he's being framed. Maybe if Steve explained or something, he could still play."

"Doug for Steve!" Beth sounded incredulous. "You really are dumb. They told me you had funny rules, but I didn't believe them. I thought I knew you. I thought you loved Claremar. I thought I meant something too." Beth's words were like chips of ice. Linda shivered.

"And listen to me, Linda," she continued. "If you *do* say a word, even a single word, I'll—I'll never speak to you again as long as I live."

"You knew," said Linda. "You've known for a long time." She looked at Beth in disbelief. "About the accident's being Steve's fault, I mean. About the beer and the way he breaks training—still. Because you knew he had beer in the car the night of our double date, didn't you? You knew about Bob too. You helped them plan. When you came by after the game—that's the night the plan began. Was it your idea, or Steve's?"

"I don't know what you're talking about." Beth sounded as though she didn't have a care in the world. "Was what my idea? To stop by your house? I've done that before. Or do you mean to get Steve's best friend to date my best friend?"

Linda looked at Beth wordlessly, then turned toward the door. Beth blocked her way. "Listen, Linda," she said, "before you go maybe you should straighten out your thinking a bit." She gave a small laugh. "Look," she said, "I'm sorry. I don't know what I was getting so dramatic about. I mean, we *are* best friends. And I'll admit it, I did want you to go to the Grid Classic with me. I *wanted* to double. It's—it's like being fixed up with a blind date, only better. I mean, isn't that what friends are for? To help?"

Linda felt as though her mind were tangled with cobwebs. This was a Beth she didn't know, this girl who changed moods quicker than you could change TV stations. "We'll be friends even if I tell?" she asked.

Beth moved away from the door and sat on her bed. She opened her hands and laid them palms up on her lap. "We're both so tense," she said. "I actually had my hands clenched."

"We'll still be friends?" Linda persisted.

"Relax," Beth said, "like I'm doing. Let's just see how things work out first. I mean, what's the hurry?"

"Doug."

"So what if he does get suspended; what's one boy to the whole school? Think of what being champs will mean."

"What if he's expelled?"

"You mean Doug?" Beth gave an impatient shrug. "So—" She leaned forward, her eyes bright with discovery. "You like him. That's what's the matter. That's why you want to be Miss Righteous. *You like Doug.*"

Linda felt her face redden. "He's just a boy, any boy. It's because now I know for sure that I have to say something. That's all."

"Uh-uh." Beth looked sure of her ground now. "You like Doug and you want to be his heroine. If it were just anybody . . ." Her voice trailed off. "But I like Steve," she continued, "I really like him. And I like Claremar, and I like our being champs, and you aren't going to do a thing." She stood up. "So help me finish the room and I'll help you get your dress."

Beth's sudden switch left Linda momentarily stunned. Then she found her words. "I have to tell," she said. "It's knowing right from wrong and doing it."

Beth shook her head. "No—not now. If you'll just think, Linda, you'll see why. Because what would you tell? That you heard a *clink?* Nobody will believe you because nobody would want to believe you. Mr. Marsh, the school, the police—we all want a championship; and we won't get it without Steve."

"You can't mean what you're saying, Beth. You just can't."

"But I do. Everybody wants a championship, no matter what. Besides, who'd go against Mr. Atkins? I mean he's . . . What do you think he'd do to your dad if you tell? He'll ruin him. That's what. Because he'll ruin anyone who gets in the way of Steve's being All-Star."

"Steve got in his own way. Can't you see that letting things go is wrong?" When Beth didn't answer, Linda tried again. "You can't shut your eyes and pretend things aren't happening."

"I guess I meant it about being friends, because, Linda, if you make trouble, I never want to speak to you again. Because if you make trouble, you'll be saying to me, 'I'll sell anyone short. I'd rather be right than be a friend.' And if that's the way you feel—"

"That's not fair. I came here, didn't I?"

"For me to sell out Steve." Beth's eyes were as cold as steel. "All I can say is you're making a mistake, and you'll be sorrier than you've ever been in your life."

Linda stood with her hand on the door knob. "I—I'm leaving, Beth," she said.

Beth turned her back to the door and switched on the vacuum.

Linda's legs felt like lead as she walked from the house and down the street. She couldn't go home. She didn't want to tell Mom, "No dance." Not yet. She walked along the streets aimlessly. What was right? What was wrong? What would Dad want her to do? Why was she so *alone* in this? She walked past the library, the city hall, the grammar school she'd attended. The warm Indian-summer sun couldn't take away her chilled, lonely feeling. She passed a church—not her church, just a church. Maybe . . .

It felt good to sink down in the last pew, alone in the quiet light. Alone, alone, alone, because she had no one to turn to. She sank to her knees and rested her head against her hands. She'd been like a pawn in Dad's chess set. Beth had used her willingly and deliberately. Now there was only the death of a friendship to mourn. The tears were wet against her hands.

CHAPTER 15

OBLIGATIONS

Linda never knew how long she stayed there in the quiet coolness of the church, kneeling, leaning against the pew. Fifteen minutes? A half hour? It didn't matter, because time was elastic. A minute could seem like forever. An hour could speed on wings. Chimes rang, an occasional person came in, an occasional person left, and Linda was aware of them as something just outside the reach of her thoughts.

After the tears had come anger—surging, shaking anger. *I should have told her off. A friend? What right had Beth to dictate? I'm free, I should have said. Maybe you're not, but I'm free. I can do what I want.*

Free? No one was free. Because there were obligations, responsibilities, duties; fetters that bound you to your school, your job, your friends, your family. No one was free—except babies, maybe. Once you became a thinking *you,* you were duty-bound. Your obligations began.

So there was no point in being mad at Beth. She had her obligations, too. It was just—which obligations were the most important? Could obligations such as those of honesty or fair play take precedence?

Bob. He'd faced his obligations the way he thought of them—Steve, Claremar, a football championship. Enough so he'd obligated himself to take her to the dance. Had he planned to drop her right afterward? Funny about Bob, because if they hadn't tried to bribe her maybe she wouldn't have known. Or did Bob think she had seen more than she had? That evening at the Hamburger Basket . . .

Was she obligated to work on Beth's campaign for grid queen? Was Beth duty-bound to keep her on?

Vickie, Mary Lou. Were they obligated to stay friends? With whom? Beth or her?

School, friends, family. Most of all she was obligated to her family, wasn't she? Like to Dad. What she did. What she said.

"Who'd go against Mr. Atkins? . . . What do you think he'd do to your Dad? . . . He'll ruin him . . ."

If she went to the authorities would Dad think that she was betraying him the way Beth thought she was a betrayer? Dad had family obligations too.

If you had a pair of old-fashioned balancing scales that could weigh obligations, how would hers balance? Because, against all other obligations, she owed one to herself. She raised her head and looked at the altar. Her lips moved silently. *"Please. Please. I want to do right."* She stood up, then, and moved quickly out of the church.

When she reached home Mom greeted her at the door. "Where have you been?" she asked. "I phoned Beth quite a while ago."

"I took the long way home."

"Obviously. Well, I guess our dress buying is off."

Linda looked started. Had Beth said something?

"If we'd started when I planned . . ." Mom broke off. "Now I have other things to do," she concluded.

Linda let out a sigh of relief. She wanted to do her own telling—to Mom and Dad together.

"I need more groceries," Mom said. "Why not fix lunch for yourself and the boys?"

Lunch? She really hadn't eaten breakfast. She was starved. As Mom hurried out the door Linda went into the kitchen. Salami, cheese, sliced tomato, French bread—one shouldn't have such an enormous appetite when one is emotionally upset, Linda told herself, but the food tasted good. After she took her last mouthful and washed it down with a gulp of milk she started on sandwiches for the twins. The screen on the back porch slammed and she looked up to see Dad and Mr. Atkins walk in.

"Your mother out?" Dad asked.

Linda nodded.

"Any coffee?" he asked.

"I'll make some fresh," Linda offered. "Sandwiches too, if you want."

"How about it, Atkins. Got time?" Dad looked at the sandwiches on the table. "Peanut butter and jam?" He wrinkled his nose.

"There's salami and cheese," Linda said. "These are for Jeff and Johnny."

"Sounds good to me," said Mr. Atkins. "You have a co-operative daughter."

"The best," Dad agreed. "My princess. What say we wash up?"

While the men were gone Linda arranged the sandwich fillers on a platter, put mayonnaise in a bowl, and stacked generous slices of crunchy French bread in the basket. By the time Dad and Mr. Atkins returned, the aroma of fresh-brewed coffee filled the kitchen.

"I thought maybe you'd perfer your own combinations," Linda said. She brought out the cups and poured the aromatic coffee.

"We're home earlier than I expected," Dad said. "Thanks, princess." He passed the bread basket to Mr. Atkins.

"Steve came out and broke up the game," Mr. Atkins said. "He—ah—he found we have a little problem to work out." He paused. "He has a nice girl, that Beth. Smart kid."

Linda's hand shook as she took cream from the refrigerator. Was Mr. Atkins trying to tell her something? He seemed to be watching her.

"Going to let your girl in on the news?" Mr. Atkins speared a tomato slice.

"Well . . ." Dad hesitated, then laughed. "I usually tell my wife first, but . . ." His eyes lit up. "We're doing the motel," he said. "Just a few wrinkles to iron out and we start building."

"Yep." Mr. Atkins grinned broadly, and his eyes seemed to be riveted on Linda. She tried to step out of their range, but it was like that picture of Sir Something-or-Other some friends had. He kept "looking" at you wherever you moved. "My lawyers are drawing up the contract now. Should be ready for your signature, Chapin, say—ah—how about the day after Thanksgiving?"

"I'll be there." Dad's elation showed in his whole bearing. This was the break he'd dreamed of. Nothing could stop him now.

Except Linda.

"The day after Thanksgiving," Mr. Atkins had said. Beth had lost no time. She must have told Steve, who had gone immediately to his dad. Nothing was to stop Steve from being All-Star—certainly not Linda. Is that what he was saying?

"We'll toast the deal with coffee. Grab yourself a cup, Linda." Mr. Atkins was the picture of amiability.

Linda poured herself a cup. Her lips felt stiff as she forced a smile and raised it.

"To the Atkins-Chapin motel," Dad toasted.

"The day after Thanksgiving," added Mr. Atkins.

He was emphasizing the point. Linda could barely swallow. The sureness she'd felt in church, the resolve she'd had en route home—they were slipping away from her. Her obligation, where did it lie? If only she could be sure of things, the way Beth was. She was like the pendulum in a grandfather clock. Tell or not, tell or not. Dad was the best contractor around. Mr. Atkins knew it. Would he really jeopardize the project because of Steve?

That long-ago first game: *"My boy will make All-Star. Nothing will stop him."* Mr. Atkins had that same gleam in his eyes now. *"The day after Thanksgiving."* Linda shuddered and put down her coffee. "I—excuse me," she said. "I've things to do." She closed the door behind her. His eyes couldn't follow a person through a wooden door. Dad. Doug. Steve. Beth. Mr. Atkins. Obligations. She went up to her room. Nothing had been solved or resolved since she'd left it to see Beth. If anything, she was more confused.

CHAPTER 16

PRESSURE POINT

The rest of the day had an unreal quality about it. There were times when Linda wondered if she weren't making a mountain out of a molehill. There were times when a strange sense of do-nothingness took over. And there were the times when sheer panic gripped her, and she felt chilled to the marrow. It was during these times that she made up her mind to say something, to talk things out with Mom and Dad.

And there was the phone call from Bob. He came right to the point. "The Grid Classic," he said. "I thought we were going."

"So you said."

"Then why the knife in the back?"

Linda didn't answer.

"I said, how come the knife in the back? I thought you liked me." Bob paused. "Okay, so I was wrong. So I thought you'd play along with Claremar. I thought you had loyalty, that you'd want a Claremar championship. So I guessed wrong again." Bob's voice became louder. "What are you, anyway? Some sort of cold fish? Or one of these holier-than-thou freaks?"

"Let's just say I'm not going to the Grid Classic."

"Come off it, Linda. I'm willing to take you to the dance

—unless you get me suspended. So be a good girl. Play ball."

"*I'm willing.*" Linda grimaced with humiliation at his words. "Thanks, Bob." She kept her voice cool and even. "But you will yourself to someone else. I'm not going to the dance." She hung up the receiver.

The phone rang. When she said, "Hello," Bob spoke rapidly. "Don't hang up until I'm through," he warned. "About the dance, I couldn't care less. About Claremar, I care a lot. And Linda, you play ball *or else.*" The phone clicked in Linda's ear and slowly she put it back into its cradle. Mr. Atkins. Bob. The word was getting around fast.

Mom and Dad had a dinner date. Linda would be twin sitting. Tim was going to Angela's after dinner, and the twins were due home at six-thirty. They were still playing ball at the park.

Several times during the afternoon Linda had been on the verge of telling Dad about the *clink*. Now, as she closed the door behind her parents, she felt as though the pressure was off for a while.

Tim came into the kitchen, clean, polished, looking very handsome. "Can I eat right now?" he asked. "I want to get going to Angela's."

"The twins will be here any minute," Linda promised. "They're late now."

"Come on, sis, I don't want to wait around." Tim settled himself at the table. "Dad said I had to be home early, anyway."

Linda hesitated and Tim pushed his chair back impatiently. "Skip it," he said. "I'll have Angela fix me something."

"I'll serve you." Linda placed a bowl of potato salad on the table. "Your hot dogs will be ready in a couple of minutes."

Four franks and rolls, two helpings of potato salad, and two glasses of milk later, Tim was ready to leave. "Good dinner," he acknowledged. "See you later."

Linda followed him to the door. "But Johnny and Jeff aren't home yet," she said.

"They don't carry clocks, do they?" Tim grinned. "Besides, they know Mom and Dad are out."

Linda watched Tim take off with long, easy strides. In a minute he'd be out of sight, enveloped in the night. It was dark. Where were the twins? They didn't need clocks to tell them it was this late. Linda closed the door, went back to the kitchen, cleared off Tim's dishes, and reset the table for the twins and herself. At least waiting didn't ruin either hot dogs or potato salad.

Now it was really dark. If they'd stopped at a friend's, wouldn't they call? Sure, they knew Mom and Dad would be out, but they could be a little thoughtful. Could they have been in an accident? Not *both*. Should she call Tim? The police? Linda paced the kitchen. She walked over to the phone, hand on the receiver, then stopped. Mom and Dad? Should she call them? Back to the kitchen . . . back to the phone . . . back and forth. The pendulum again. . . . The door burst open. And the twins were home.

Linda felt her fear turn to hot rage. "Where were you?" she stormed. "Look at the time. I'm telling Mom and Dad." And then she saw them—*really* saw them. They looked on the verge of tears, only big boys don't cry. Jeff's shirt was torn, Johnny's left eye swollen almost shut. "What happened?"

"They said you were a stool pigeon, a rat." Jeff blurted out the words. "We tried to fight, only they were big guys."

Linda's knees felt like limp spaghetti. She sank into a chair. "What are you talking about? What boys? Bob? You mean Bob?"

"We're not saying." Johnny looked at her steadily with his one good eye. "Or we'd be stool pigeons. They said so."

"They said people should play ball with Claremar. What's that mean?" asked Jeff. "They said to tell you."

"They *who*," Linda demanded. She was up on her feet now, and she grabbed Jeff by the shoulders. "Bob? Steve?"

Jeff broke her grasp and moved out of reach. "Their friends," he said coldly. "That's all we're saying. But why aren't you saying you're not a stool pigeon?"

"You're not, are you?" Johnny insisted. "You're not what they said, are you?"

"No," she said. "I'm not." She felt the tears very near. But big girls shouldn't cry either. "Clean up for supper, okay?"

She felt grim as she heated the dinner—grim with despair. *They* were applying pressure where it would work best, through her family.

As the twins ate, they began to swagger with self-importance. They'd been gallant knights, protecting her honor. From whom? They wouldn't say. Perhaps it was better, not having names named, until she talked to Mom and Dad. She gave Johnny an ice pack for his eye.

137

The twins were in bed but still talking when the phone rang. Linda picked up the receiver.

"Tim there?"

"No," she answered. "Who's calling?"

"Jeff and John there?"

"Yes," she said. "Who's calling?"

"Just something to think about." She heard the phone go dead. Tim. Was it to be Tim's turn next? Maybe she should call up right now and say she'd play ball. Maybe she should call Tim and warn him.

Dining room, hall, living room, and back again. Linda paced. And she wavered. Tim would be furious if she phoned him at Angela's. And if she didn't? Dining room, hall, living room— She heard someone come up the walk, heard a key in the door. Tim. She hurried to him.

"You all right?"

Tim backed off from her concern. "Sure. I'm not even late. What's the matter with you?"

They'd been teasing her, cat-and-mouse fashion. Tim was as jaunty and assured as ever. She gave a small laugh. "Nerves," she said.

"Girls!" Tim yawned. "Guess I'll hit the sack."

Linda felt confused. It had been a devastating day. She'd lost a friend, declined a bribe (the Grid Classic), faced another (Dad's contract), the twins were roughed up, and there was the evasive call. Somehow, right now, an awful lot was at stake. Linda prepared for bed, trying to list her thoughts into pros and cons.

Suppose she turned "stool pigeon," as the twins so crudely put it? What would she say?

Steve was to blame for the accident. (Proof: Vickie had witnessed his wild driving too.)

Bob planted beer in Doug's car. (Proof: the *clink*; she'd *seen* Bob by Doug's car; and she'd been bribed by the dance.) *Oh, come now, Linda, try to prove that.*

To whom should she go?

Mr. Marsh? The coach? The police? *"Nobody would believe you because nobody would want to believe you."* Beth's words this morning. It seemed so long ago.

Say they *did* believe. Then what?

Steve, Bob, and others in the car would be suspended.

Claremar would lose the championship.

Steve would lose All-Star.

And Dad would lose his contract.

She would be regarded by her football town as a traitor, and her infamy would rub off on Tim and the twins —even on Mom and Dad. And what about the *Clarion*, the exchange program? What about *friends*?

If she could just wait until after Thanksgiving. . . . That would be too late. She would appear merely stupid. Even now time was running short. Her motive might be suspect, as Beth believed. She'd thought that Doug was Linda's reason. He was, but not as Beth saw him. Not as Doug *personally*, but as Doug the scapegoat who was caught in a web of circumstantial evidence that was false. Doug had become a puppet on a string. Only he wasn't the *only* puppet. Claremar was a town of puppets with Mr. Atkins pulling the strings.

Linda heard her parents come in and check to see that the boys were home. Dad opened her door softly, peeked in. He saw that her eyes were open and tiptoed over.

"'Night, princess," he said. "Sweet dreams." He leaned down and kissed her and walked quietly out.

It was such a comfortable feeling, knowing her parents were home. It was a *safe* feeling. Dad wasn't a puppet, no matter what. Parents were for problems. Sometimes they were Mom problems, sometimes they were Dad problems. This was a Dad problem. She'd give it to him tomorrow, let him take over. She snuggled down under her blankets. The pressure was off. Let Dad do it. Only one niggling doubt. Dad would see this was a matter of integrity, of honor, of justice, wouldn't he? He wouldn't be contract-blinded, would he? Linda blocked out the doubt as she drifted toward sleep.

CHAPTER 17

STORM WARNING

Sunday was overcast. The family attended church as usual, although Johnny hadn't wanted to go. His eye was still swollen, but Mom, who accepted his explanation of a "slight disagreement," had insisted. Linda saw the several amused, questioning glances Johnny was subject to, and felt guilty. But things had been too rushed, too confused to have a serious talk with Dad before church. Everything should have its right moment, and Linda willingly awaited hers.

The day took on a brooding look. The sky turned a darker gray, and the breeze turned into a wind. "Storm's on the way," Dad said as he and the boys removed the last of the screens for winter storing and did all the other chores Dad deemed necessary.

Winter? It wasn't even Thanksgiving. She was rushing things. But she wondered what her life would be like, say, a month from now. She felt the twins watching her. They were staying pretty close to home, she noticed. Tim too. Or was this because Dad was demanding of their time?

Linda felt restless. She tried to study, but the words didn't make much sense. She had better luck when she worked on an editorial, although it sounded much too personal. She missed Beth's phone calls. She missed Vickie and Mary Lou. Didn't her parents notice how seldom the phone rang today? It would provide such a nice opportunity to start her story if they would. How good it was going to feel to tell!

Later in the afternoon her grandparents dropped in, and Mom persuaded them to stay for dinner. Linda usually enjoyed her grandparents' visits but today she was anxious for them to leave. Dinner was a prolonged, jovial time. The air was peppered with "remember whens?" and when Dad told about the motel, Grandpa recalled the very first "auto courts," which were slightly better than shacks.

"Fifty units will be a big job," Grandpa concluded.

"And he's the man to do it," Mom said. She looked proud and happy, and Linda felt her spirits drop.

The air had a storm *smell* to it, Linda decided, as they stood at the door, saying their farewells to Grandma and Grandpa.

"Rain any minute," Grandpa predicted. "Hope I get home before it starts."

"Drive carefully," Dad warned. "Remember, the first rain makes a dangerous oil slick on the streets."

Grandpa grinned as he started the motor. "You're like your mother," he said. "A real back-seat driver."

The twins were already in bed, Dad and Mom had decided to watch a certain TV program, and still Linda hadn't got around to telling about Steve and Doug. She had waited all day for the right moment. She began to wonder if right moments ever came, or if you had to create them.

Tim stood in the doorway. "I'm going to bed," he announced. He paused. "Remember what I said yesterday about Doug? Listen to this. His mom's a drunk. She's here for the cure or something. They're living with her sister because she was wrecking his dad's job. Angela told me last night. All the kids know." He saluted them. "'Night," he said.

For a moment Tim's words took her breath away, as he used to when they were younger and he'd sock her in the stomach. Now, as then, sudden anger made her want to hit back, but not at Tim, who was merely repeating what he'd heard, but at the others—the ones who'd started the rumor. What a dirty way to play, to spread stories like *that*. Rumors had such a deadly ooze to them. She'd seen Doug's mother at the Hamburger Basket—timid, unsure, but *not drunk*.

"Poor boy." Mom sighed. "What a shame!"

"He's had it rough," Dad added.

Linda stared at her parents in disbelief. They'd accepted Tim's gossip as fact. They weren't even questioning it. She reined her thoughts, sharply. They didn't know that's why; they didn't know the facts. She took a deep breath. "Maybe, Dad," she said, "you can help Doug." She tried to choose her words carefully as she explained. The accident, the *clink* and Bob at the car, the "bribe," the twins' fight, the phone calls, even Mr. Atkins and the contract. She kept her eyes on the rug as she talked. "See what they're doing?" she concluded. "Now they're attacking his mother. Mr. Atkins wants Steve to make All-Star so bad, he'll stop at nothing."

Mom had turned off the TV as Linda talked. Now a quietness filled the room, as she waited for Dad to say something. He'd hunched over, hands clasped, studying their backs or the floor. He looked up, met her gaze. The silence continued taut, like a rubber band stretched to its capacity.

Linda broke it. "What can we do?" she asked. "Now what?"

"You've made ugly accusations, Linda. You frighten me." Dad got to his feet. "I—frankly, I don't know where to begin."

Linda felt relief surge through. She knew it. Dad was wonderful. Dad was taking over.

"I don't see how you got started," he continued. "You've been so sensible, so levelheaded. And now you think that every move, every act in the whole community is suspect. Why? Why are you misinterpreting?"

Linda stared at her father. It was as if he'd suddenly become a stranger. "You don't believe me! You didn't believe a word I said. You're not taking me seriously!"

"I *am* taking you seriously. That's the trouble. Accusations are serious, dangerous things."

"Then why won't you help?"

"I believe in your sincerity, Linda, but you're way off base."

"Is it fair to call somebody's mother a drunk? You heard Tim."

" 'Drunk' is an ugly word. I—"

"They're saying it to smear him." Linda interrupted her dad. "Don't you see? So he'd have reason for the beer."

Dad held up his hand as if to stop her words. "Just a minute, Linda, just a minute. First of all, accept the fact that alcoholism does exist—in suburbs as well as cities, among women as well as men, in mothers as well as fathers. And sometimes in the very best of families."

"So just because they say—I mean, you think—"

"I think Tim was wrong to repeat gossip. I was wrong

144

to accept it, and you are wrong to consider it more than just gossip, which is bad enough."

"You don't think they're trying to smear Doug, give him a reason?"

"If Mrs. Johnson is alcoholic, it seems to me Doug would be less likely to drink."

"What about Johnny's eye? What about—about Bob—and the dance?"

"I'm inclined to think Johnny was 'defending honor,' as he said. You do have some importance in school. Now, suddenly, you are filled with accusations—"

"And I just know Beth would never hurt you," Mom interrupted. "You've been friends too long."

You weren't there, Linda thought. *You didn't hear Beth.*

"As I recall," Dad said, "kids have a code—at least they did when I was a boy. You didn't run afoul of the rules. You stuck together."

Linda knew about "kids' codes." They'd probably always exist. It was a way kids had of taking care of their own problems. And they could be as relentless, sometimes, as the Ku Klux Klan. But this was more; this was action directed by Mr. Atkins, she was sure. And it wasn't "just kids" involved. Mr. Atkins—he pulled a string. His puppets performed.

"You don't think Mr. Atkins threatened me?"

"With the contract?" Dad gave a rueful laugh. "No, I'm afraid not. I agree, though; he does enjoy keeping people dangling. There's no good reason we couldn't have the contract sooner. It's going to mean a lot to us."

Dad didn't want to see. He wanted the contract so badly, he refused to see.

"You'd hate me. Everyone would," Linda stated flatly.

"Linda!" Mom's voice was shocked.

"I'd never *hate* you, Linda," Dad said gently, "I just don't want anybody hurt. If you persist, if you insist, just be very sure of your grounds, and go to the right source."

"What's that—the right source?"

"You'll have to figure that out for yourself."

"I thought you'd help." Linda stood up and faced both her parents. "I thought you'd want to help. But you won't. You're scared. You might lose the contract. Everybody else is scared. We might lose a championship. Nobody cares about just a—a person. People don't matter any more," she stormed, "just importance." Her eyes blazed. "What if you don't get the contract? What then?"

"That," her father said calmly, "is a bridge I'll cross when I get to it. We are existing, you know. Right now. We do get along. We manage."

"I'm going to bed." Linda jutted her jaw defiantly.

"Perhaps things will look more reasonable in the morning," Dad said. "So kiss us good night."

More reasonable in the morning? Why didn't Dad just come out and say, "See it my way," which of course would be more "reasonable." Linda climbed into bed and tugged at the blankets angrily. Dad had changed. Everything he'd taught them about honor and integrity, all those things— they didn't count for anything when it came to importance. Or was it something more tangible, like money? Mr. Atkins had it. And he'd mesmerized the town.

Linda reached over to switch out her lamp. She brushed against a book and it fell to the floor. She leaned over, glanced at it, and let it lay. *U. S. History*. She'd pick it up in the morning. Now she lay in the darkness, her thoughts swirling around like a washing machine on "spin dry." It was true about Mr. Atkins' being the big man in town. He *did* boss, *did* control. *Boss Tweed.* Hadn't he run New York City *his* way almost a hundred years ago? Of course Mr. Atkins wasn't that big. Claremar wasn't New York. But he controlled. He had his finger in everything. Something—someone—had to stop him. How? When? Where? Who? Linda felt her thoughts whirl into nothingness as she drifted off to sleep.

The storm must have blown in about three. Linda woke to the slash of rain against the window. She snuggled down into her covers for a few minutes, then got up and knelt by the window. It was a raging, angry storm, the first of the season. The wind whipped at the trees, sending the last of the browned leaves to the ground, and she remembered the story of *Bambi,* and how the two leaves conversed. The water swirled around storm holes, ink-black in the shimmer of the street lamp. Storms were fun to watch when you were snug and safe. She saw the branch of an elm crash to the street. She shivered. Storms always did some damage. In the daylight the block would have a shaken-down look. The trees would be stripped to their essentials. Nature had a way of taking care of things. And when she attacked, she always forewarned.

Linda rested her chin on her arm as she watched. The wind was abating. It still came in sudden gusts, whipping along sheets of rain. In between gusts the rain pelted the ground steadily, irrevocably.

The other storm that was brewing, which one of them was the elm? Which one would be broken?

CHAPTER 18

ALIEN TERRITORY

Linda shivered. Pre-dawns were chilling affairs. She pulled a blanket from her bed to wrap around her and heard books fall to the floor. She switched on her lamp. Besides history, there was now her binder, her lit book, and another. As she started to replace it, she noted the title. It was about courage, written by the late President Kennedy when he'd been senator. Dad had suggested it for her next history book report, said it would counteract the Tweeds. Courage? She could do with some. She leafed through and saw that the chapter heads were quotes from the "men of courage." One in particular . . . She checked back to the chapter's beginning. Senator Lucius Lamar had said it, back in the 1870s. "Today I must be true or false." She repeated the words to herself. *Today I must be true or false.* Another time she'd find out why he said them. But now—

Today, she, Linda Chapin, must be true. If no one wanted to believe, she would have to make them. It wasn't just because a boy's well-being was at stake. It was a matter of honor and integrity for so many. Today she would have to have determination and the courage of her convictions. She couldn't vacillate, be a pendulum. Not if today she would be true.

Her first step would be an editorial. She'd take it at

noon to the printshop as a substitute for the innocuous one she'd written. The *Clarion* came out tomorrow. She stuck a sheet of paper into the typewriter, and as she wrote she forgot about the cold.

By the time the alarm clock in her parents' room sounded, Linda was well started on the day. Her bed was made, her clothes put away, she was dressed, and her editorial was something she was proud of. It hadn't been easy to write—the crumpled papers in her wastebasket were proof of that. But now she wondered why the words didn't burn holes in the paper as she stressed the American way of honesty and integrity and pointed up a few ways both faculty and students might "clean house." The editorial was the best writing she'd ever done. It was also her obituary—because once it came out, she would no longer be associated with the *Clarion*. She was going over the heads of Mr. Hall and Mr. Marsh, who insisted that material for the paper be checked by them. But, since they belonged to the clique who "refused to see," she had no choice.

The early fury of the storm had spent itself, and now the rain was a mere drizzle. Breakfast conversation was carefully channeled into topics as safe as the weather and last night's storm. Tim and the twins had already gone to school when Linda realized that she was living in the past. Beth wouldn't be picking her up any more.

"I'll drive you," Mom said. "Or, better yet, you drive Dad to the station, and then you can have the car. I won't need it today."

She kissed Mom good-by and followed Dad to the car, where she slid behind the wheel, started the motor, and let it warm up a bit.

Traffic was heavy at the station. Dad slipped out of the car quickly. "Chin up, princess," he said. "Things will work out." Linda didn't quite catch his last words, but it sounded as if he said something about "faith in you." The train was on its way before she extricated herself from the traffic jam. *"Faith in you."* Was this his final pitch *not* to tell? But today she must be true. She had her editorial to bolster her resolve.

The student parking lot was full of cars, void of students. She'd have to park near the school. The late bell must have rung. Perhaps she should cut first period and see Mr. Marsh. *Before* she took in the editorial? Dad had said last night to "go to the right source" if she persisted. Was Mr. Marsh the right source? A source was a beginning, a cause. Just what was the beginning? The accident. Steve. His dad. Go to Mr. Atkins? The thought was electrifying, scary. But she was late already. She could drive to his office, and afterward she could tell Mom and get an excuse.

Linda stopped at a service station to look up the address. It was on a San Francisco street she knew, thank goodness. Before she turned onto the freeway she drove by the printer's and dropped her editorial into the mail slot. Now there was no turning back.

No wonder Dad took the train to work. Even though the main traffic peak was over, the freeway still had pockets of bumper-to-bumper cars. The city's maze of one-way streets, a near-to-the-office parking lot, and Linda finally arrived at the right building. She held tight to her resolution as she walked into the lobby and read the directory. The elevator whisked her upward much too fast, and there she was, facing the door with the bold gold lettering. She could still leave and no one would know the difference. She gripped the doorknob firmly. Turn. Push. Step. The door clicked shut behind her.

"I'd like to see Mr. Atkins," she told the receptionist.

"You've an appointment? Your name?"

"Please. Just tell him Linda Chapin is here."

"Just a moment." The receptionist looked doubtful. She gestured Linda toward a chair. "Mr. Atkins isn't in right now."

Linda picked the only straight-backed chair in the room—*to stiffen my backbone,* she told herself. She clutched her purse to keep from fidgeting. Who did she think she was, coming here like this? Maybe she should leave. She was just an unimportant, insignificant kid. Mr. Atkins was important. His office reflected it. He was king. At least she wasn't one of his puppets; he didn't have her on a string.

"Mr. Atkins will see you now."

Linda started, then stood up. Her legs felt weak. She walked into the inner office.

Mr. Atkins' welcoming smile didn't go as far as his eyes. They were flint-hard. "Well, my dear, a surprise." He offered the chair across from him.

Linda sat gingerly on the edge of the chair. Mr. Atkins was waiting for her to say something. She opened her mouth, closed it, opened it again—*like a fish,* Linda thought frantically. "It's the accident," she blurted. "I've come about that."

"Oh?"

"Steve was to blame. You know that."

"You seem pretty sure of yourself, my dear."

"He's framing someone. Doug. You know that."

151

"So?"

"It's wrong—very wrong. I have to tell Mr. Marsh it was Steve's beer in Doug's car."

Mr. Atkins leaned back in his chair and pressed the tips of his fingers together. "Do you have proof?"

"I heard Bob put it in."

Mr. Atkins riveted his gaze on her. "Does your father know you're here?"

Linda shook her head. "But I told him what I thought last night. He thinks I'm at school."

"We've an important business arrangement pending, your dad and I."

"We toasted it Saturday."

"Yet you came here. Do you think I'd want to do business with a family who accused my son?"

"Dad isn't accusing anybody."

"You, his daughter, are. Do you think your dad would be happy about that? This deal is well worth his while."

Linda shook her head. Dad wouldn't be happy, but he'd understand, she hoped. "I had to come," Linda stated. "And Dad—he loves me. He has faith in me. He even said so."

"I love Steve." Mr. Atkins leaned forward, his eyes fierce. "Steve is my life. I want the world for him. I'll give him the world. I want him proud, admired. When he's All-Star, he'll have something no one can ever take from him. He'll be a hero." Mr. Atkins placed his hands palm down on his desk. "When I was in high I served on the football team too." He glared at her, his mouth an ugly sneer. "I was water boy. *How many can you name?*"

Linda shrank against the chair, trying to escape his bitterness.

"Steve will be All-Star." He leaned back in his chair. "What I don't understand is how you'd sell your team, your school, even your family short for somebody so insignificant. Don't you have feelings?" His gaze was speculative. "Maybe it's just the female of the species. Mrs. Atkins doesn't want things like I do. Maybe girls never want things bad enough."

Girls *did* want things. And they worked for them—as she did on the paper and for the exchange-student program. It was just . . .

"Or maybe," Mr. Atkins continued, "you're one of those natural-born reformers—offensive creatures at best." He paused. "The authorities won't listen. They won't believe you."

Linda stood up. "I have to try," she said. "That's why I came here, to tell you I have to try."

"Sit down." Mr. Atkins barked the order. "I'll ruin your dad, that I promise. You start trouble, I'll ruin him." He glared. "Have you any idea of my importance in Claremar?"

Linda nodded. "I still have to tell." Her voice wasn't much above a whisper. "Because of Doug," she went on. "But more because of Steve—and you."

"Me?"

"No one is important to you, not even Steve, really. You have to be king. You have to run things, pull strings." Linda paused. Her voice was stronger with each word. Her hands ached, and she realized that she was clutching her purse so her knuckles showed white. She tried to relax her hold. "You won't admit people are *people*. We're just your puppets. Even Steve."

"You—" Mr. Atkins almost sputtered. "You— Steve is no puppet. Down on the field he plays his heart out. No one's pulling any strings."

"He's playing to be All-Star for you. And you *do* pull strings, because he knows he can do anything and get away with it—like not getting tickets when he should. He's a crazy driver, you know."

"All boys are crazy drivers. It's part of being a boy."

"Not really. Not as bad as Steve, anyway." Linda paused. "You know something," she said finally, "you cheat Steve. No matter what happens, you're there. My dad—well, if Tim or I or anyone makes a mistake, Dad lets us fight our way out. It's like—" Linda groped for words. "Once Dad read us an ad in the "personals" column of the paper. If you wanted to be a great artist, all you did was contact this fellow, tell him the picture you wanted to paint, he'd do it for you, and you signed your name. Just like that. And that's what you're doing to Steve. You're trying to do a picture of his life, and he gets to sign his name." She forced herself to look straight at Mr. Atkins. The things she was saying—they shocked her. She *was* being offensive.

Mr. Atkins brushed aside her words with an impatient gesture. "The authorities can't afford to believe you," he said. "Your dad can't afford to have you talk. I—" The phone rang and he picked up the receiver. He answered in monosyllables, and Linda had the impression that she was intruding. She looked around the room, trying to show her unconcern. The clock on Mr. Atkins' desk—she'd been in the room less than fifteen minutes.

As Mr. Atkins hung up his gaze was speculative. "I'll make a bargain with you," he said, "a twenty-four-hour bargain during which you'll do nothing and say nothing."

"I can't."

Mr. Atkins ignored her protest. "Just twenty-four hours. You give me the time, and I promise to sign your dad's contract. Just one day, and you go to the authorities as you plan."

Linda watched him, puzzled. What could he do in twenty-four hours? He couldn't change facts.

"You'll still have time to present your accusations, Linda. Surely you can see that." Mr. Atkins stood up and Linda followed suit. He held out his hand. "A bargain, Linda, to shake on. You won't tell anyone—*anyone* you were here. Okay?"

"Ever?"

"Twenty-four hours. Shake?"

Linda hesitated, then gave him hers. Twenty-four hours wasn't an eternity. Nothing would be changed by tomorrow—not really.

She felt that she was being dismissed and walked to the door. As she opened it Mr. Atkins called to her. She turned.

"That was your dad on the phone," he said. "Don't be too sure *he* doesn't dabble in paints once in a while."

She closed the door behind her.

CHAPTER 19

COUNT DOWN

Linda stopped at a tiny lunch counter on her way to the car. She sipped her Coke, trying for composure. Had she been wrong—to have a twenty-four-hour truce? Or was it a compromise? It was going to be difficult to get Mom to write an excuse. And the longer she waited, the more difficult it would be. Linda gulped the last swallows, paid, and hurried to the car.

The sun was shining when she turned onto the freeway. Black clouds hung over the horizon, but it was sunny now. Linda rolled down the window all the way. There was such a good clean *freshness* to the air after the first rain. Traffic was light now, and Linda picked up speed. She saw a patrol car head in the opposite direction and automatically checked the speedometer. She was okay. She pulled to the right for the Claremar turn-off when she caught sight of a second patrol car in her rear-view mirror. This one was bearing down on her, signal flashing, the siren parting the air with its wail. She pulled to the side to let it pass. Only it didn't go on. It parked directly in front of her, and the patrolman got out and came over.

"Okay?" he asked. "Alone?"

Linda nodded. Her voice seemed to have deserted her.

"License checks. Let's see yours."

Linda dug in her purse for her wallet, flipped it open to her driver's license. Her hands were shaking.

"Name?"

"It's there. Linda Chapin."

"Follow me."

Linda felt panic clutch at her as she fell in behind the patrol car. Twenty-four hours. Mr. Atkins— But no, the car was turning toward her home. A second police car was in front of her home. *Something terrible had happened.* She flung open the door and tore up the sidewalk to burst into the house. "Mom," she cried, "Mom, what is it?"

Her mother clutched her, clung to her. "You're safe. You're all right," she kept repeating.

"If you don't mind, Mrs. Chapin."

Linda looked up at the voice, aware of the blue-uniformed man standing in the hallway.

"Thank you, *thank you* for bringing her home safe." Mom's voice was shaky.

"What is it, Mom?" Linda repeated. "What happened?"

"Where have been?" Mom asked. "Ever since the school called, I've been frantic."

The school. She'd forgotten about the ever-efficient attendance office. When the first attendance report went in . . .

Linda swallowed. "I went for a ride."

"You went for a *ride!*" Mom's words were like ice cubes. "Just that?"

"Caught up with her turning off the freeway, ma'am," the patrolman offered.

"I drove to the city—I mean, when I was driving around, I—"

"Why?"

"I—I felt like it."

"Go to your room." Mom's voice was a whiplash.

Linda felt her face flush at Mom's order. She was being treated like a child, but she was glad to escape. *Twenty-four hours was going to be a long time. She had twenty-three left.*

The police finally left, and Linda heard her mother talking on the phone, then just routine house noises, and then, finally she heard Mom's footsteps coming up the stairs. Mom walked into the room and dumped Linda's binders and books onto the bed. "Well?"

"I—I went for a ride, that's all."

Mom turned wordlessly and walked downstairs.

Linda lay on her bed and watched the second hand of the clock tick itself around the dial. One minute, two minutes, three—four—she could match the seconds by counting one hundred and one, one hundred and two— A complete waste of time, but she had almost twenty-three hours to kill. Around and around and around . . .

"Well, Linda?"

Dad's voice made Linda sit up with a start. She'd dozed. *That* long? She looked quickly at the clock. *Just one.*

"I came home from the office as soon as I could. You gave your mother a bad time."

"I'm sorry."

"She thought, because of your wild accusations last night, that—" Dad broke off. "Where did you go? And why?"

"I—I wanted to. I—at the time I wanted to. That's all."

"This is the only explanation you are giving?"

Linda nodded.

"I can't understand you. All of a sudden you've changed." Dad's eyes looked hurt. Then they hardened. "But I can say this. You will not drive the car again this year."

This year! Linda watched helplessly as Dad walked away. She was doing very well—a police escort, no more car, and at school, as these hours ticked off, she was earning big fat Fs. Mr. Atkins was getting the better of the deal, no matter what.

The afternoon wore on. Linda opened her history text and tried to study. She was hungry. Either Mom had forgotten about her lunch, or was trying to starve her. She wandered about the room. Was she "confined to quarters" until Mom or Dad released her? Long ago, life was much simpler. You stood up for what you believed in, and that was that. Except that "fors" always have "againsts," which meant that some people stood up for what was *wrong*. Which meant that she'd better concentrate on the War of 1812.

Some people were bird watchers. Linda decided that she was a clock watcher. The twins came home on schedule and went out again. She heard the doorbell—and a new male voice talk to Dad. There was something about the voice— She caught her breath to listen.

"Linda!" Dad called.

"Coming!" Linda applied fresh lipstick and combed her hair with hurried strokes. *Did she look okay? What was he doing here?*

Dad and Doug stood in the hall and watched her descent.

"Doug has a serious matter to discuss. Wants to take you for a walk. I said 'okay,' if you want to go."

Mind? Didn't Dad *mind*? After keeping her in her room all afternoon?

"Please, Linda?" Doug asked.

Be indifferent, aloof. Remember, you couldn't care less. Linda shrugged. "Okay, I guess."

"It's chilly. Wear a sweater," Mom commanded.

Back in her room, Linda grabbed her sweater—blue, for her eyes; wasn't it convenient it went with what she was wearing?—and made a swift check of her appearance. Her glance swept the clock. *Tempus* certainly didn't *fugit* today, but at least time was marching on. Her twenty-four hours —*did Mr. Atkins have something to do with Doug's being here?*

Doug held open the front door for her. "I'll be back in just a little while," she told her parents.

There was a hint of a drizzle, and the streets were wet. That feel of winter penetrated, and Linda shivered. The drizzle was a bit stronger. They walked on. *He'd* have to break the silence first.

"Great day for ducks," Doug commented. "It is, you know," he continued. "Rain doesn't bother them. They have a water-resistant substance in their feathers—that is, if they're raised naturally. However, if they're incubator-raised, the substance isn't there and they even—"

Linda giggled. Two blocks of walking in the rain and he talks about *ducks*. "Is that why you came over today? To talk about *ducks*?"

"No. Not quite." Doug's shoulders looked hunched in his bulky sweater. His hands were thrust deep into his pockets, and his face had a strained look about it. Their glances met and a brief smile caught at his lips. "I thought it would be easy. It isn't," he said.

"What isn't?"

"Just—just don't go to bat for me, Linda. I'm expendable. You're not."

Linda bristled. Of all the conceit! Then the full impact of Doug's words hit her, and she felt ill. *Mr. Atkins. Doug, selling out.* She drew away.

"Don't get mad." Doug reached out, took her hand, and drew her back to his side. "I—maybe I put it wrong. It's just—you *belong* to Claremar, like your folks belong to the town. I don't. You're a part of things. I'm not."

"Even *you're* against me." Linda felt tears sting her eyes. "Even you *forget* for a price." She tried to free her hand.

"Maybe. If you put it that way, maybe." He kept a firm grasp. "The park—it's over a block. Let's—let's see if there's a dry bench. I—I want to explain."

"I want to go home."

"Ten more minutes, Linda. Just ten?"

Ten minutes—twenty-four hours. What was time, anyway? Besides, this was Mr. Atkins' time. Could you give the same time to different people? An editorial, that. Ho. The one she'd turned in to Mr. Benning this morning sure was wasted effort. She shrugged, and matched Doug's strides.

The benches were damp, so she leaned against a fat oak, sheltered from the drizzle, and listened. The sun's rays showed weakly, and a faint rainbow curved in the distance.

"You'll get hurt," Doug said. "If you bother with me, that is. You—you'll probably make editor next year. But, face it, Claremar's a football school. And your town is a football town. Jeopardize that—you're through."

"Was the beer yours?"

Doug shook his head.

"Then I'm through if I don't. Because it isn't *you*, it's honor and integrity."

"You can't buck a school or a town. The kids'll hate you." Doug paused. "If you let things ride," he continued, "they'll work out. They always do. And you won't get hurt. You've taken enough chances already. When I heard the scuttlebutt I had to talk to you, see you. I waited outside English, only you didn't come." He held her hand, palm up. "I like your hands," he said. "Long, slender fingers, strong, but delicate too. Piano fingers, my aunt would say. Only you play the typewriter with them instead. You play words."

He turned her hand over and clasped it firmly in his, palms together. Linda felt odd, as though her hand didn't belong to her any more, that it was Doug's; it belonged in his clasp. But she *couldn't* feel this way. Not when Doug was selling out.

"Maybe," Doug was saying, "maybe—if things were different, if I played football here, we'd be doubling with your friend Beth for the Grid Classic. Don't I wish!" His laugh was short and bitter. *"Student participation.* Remember that editorial?"

Linda reddened. That editorial was forever linked to her humiliation over the Fall Frolic. "Something you don't believe in," she said. *Now* her hand didn't belong in his.

"I wanted to take you to that dance more than anything

162

else in the world. I even figured how you'd have time to ask. And then—something just blew up."

"Forget it. It's not important."

"It *is* important. It's the reason I'm living in Claremar instead of down South." Doug drew a deep breath. He let go of her hand and dug his own deep in his pockets. "The houses we passed walking here looked like secure, happy homes, didn't they?"

Linda nodded.

"That's the way ours looked too—on the outside. Only inside it was miserable. My dad's a coach—high-school football. I grew up on it. I played it—down there. My sister—she's in nurse's training now—she and I learned to be pretty cagey about our house. We didn't dare have kids over because they might find out. Sometimes we had to stay home from school. Some days Dad did. To take care of Mom. We kept things pretty well under cover, or so we thought. And then things got worse. Or rather Mom did. Much worse."

Linda wanted to stretch out her hand, take Doug's. She wanted to lay her finger on his lips, hush his hurt, bitter words. Or maybe she should just listen. The thin wail of a siren sounded in the distance. Someone was in trouble.

"Do you know what I'm trying to tell you, Linda? My mother is ill. Back home people politely say she had a nervous breakdown and is now recuperating. It's a pleasant cover-up for Dad, I guess, so he can go on with his job. But they know what we knew. She drinks." He looked at her as though he expected her to recoil. "She drinks," he repeated. "And the week before the Fall Frolic she went on a bender. When you asked me to the dance, I knew I couldn't go, but I didn't know how to explain."

"You live with your aunt?"

"Yes. Mom's older sister. She wrote about the clinic near here. Mom's trying to take the cure. I'm around so she knows she's still loved." Doug look spent, drained.

"At the Hamburger Basket that night, was that your—"

"My mother. She's a nice person, Linda, someone you really like when she's okay. And then she'll 'take just a thimbleful' is the way she puts it—and we've had it. It's not that I don't love her. I do. It's just—well, she's the one who pours it and picks it up and drinks it, that thimbleful, even when she knows what it's going to do. If she could just figure the *why*, the reason. . . ." He stretched out his hand. "So now you know," he said. "I'll take you home."

"Dad says alcoholism is—"

"Your dad knows about my mother?"

"Not really. Tim repeated a rumor."

"A rumor." Doug repeated the words. "I'm surprised your dad let you come out with me if he thinks I carry beer and—and Mom drinks."

She'd been surprised too.

"Now you see why you shouldn't get into this mess. So stay out. Okay?" Doug kept his voice light.

"I don't see what you said that makes the difference. If you are expelled for someone else's act, if you're sued—"

"I'm insured. Dad made sure of that when I got my first permit."

"Expellings too? He has you covered for that?"

"Look, Linda, for your sake don't get involved. You live

164

here. Claremar is your town because you're going to keep on living here. You have hopes. But me—I'm a newcomer, a nobody. Sure, I resented it when they first pinned all the blame on me. But now—"

And now Mr. Atkins had reached him. Was that it? Was this a part of the twenty-four-hour truce she'd made?

"Promise me, Linda, please, that you'll just go on being you, and forget about all this. Okay?"

"I told you. It's a matter of honor and integrity. I can't just shrug it away."

"But can't you see it's enough that I know, you know, and—and my dad knows too—that I wasn't to blame? So Steve needs a scapegoat and I'm it. If I could buck it alone, okay. But not with you. You've got too much to lose. You want to be editor. You want to go to France. Your chances are good—for both. But not if you take on Mr. Atkins. Believe me." They'd turned up her front walk now and were standing by the door. "If you won't stay out for your sake then how about for mine? Okay?"

"For your sake?" Linda repeated. "I—I—"

The front door opened before she could complete her thought.

"Door locked or something?" Jeff asked. "You've stood here so long."

"See you, Linda," Doug said. He turned abruptly and walked off.

Linda entered the house and Jeff closed the door. His rudeness had been uncalled for, but he'd saved her from answering Doug.

"It's about time, princess," Dad said. "Wash up for dinner. It's later than you think." Dad's smile told her she was back in the family again—at least temporarily.

As she washed up she considered Doug's strange attitude. He *must* have sold out to Mr. Atkins. *What were the terms?* she wondered. Financial help, maybe, for his mother's cure? Mr. Atkins worked so fast. And Doug, so willing to back down. "For your sake"—and then, more honestly, "for my sake."

"Step on it, sis," Tim bellowed up the stairs. "I'm starved."

Starved? Actually, she was pretty hungry herself. It was a long time since that Coke in the city. She took her place at the table. Dad served, and she felt as if she could hardly wait to start. She wanted to attack her food the way Tim did. *Tim.* He'd begun this train of events last night with his rumor. Doug called it "scuttlebutt." His words came back to her: "When I heard the scuttlebutt, I had to talk to you, see you. I waited outside English, only you didn't come." Weren't those his words? And she hadn't been there because she was on her way to the city. That meant—it meant *Doug hadn't sold out.* He—he really was trying to save her. She felt herself grin like a Cheshire cat at her family. *Doug.* Just thinking the name gave her a tingly feeling. After dinner she'd tell Dad and Mom what Doug had tried to do. And nothing, just nothing, could beat mashed potatoes and gravy for taste

I love my family, she thought as she listened to them talk. The phone rang. Tim got up to answer it. "We're having dinner, Tim," Mom warned.

In two minutes he was back. "That was Vickie," he said. "Beth's in the hospital. She's been hurt bad. A car accident —with Steve."

Linda's world rocked crazily. She couldn't breathe.

CHAPTER 20

VIGIL

Hospitals were so busy. Everyone had a job—except the *you* placed unimportantly in a waiting room. You twiddled, or leafed unseeingly through a magazine, or paced like a caged animal, the way Beth's father did. Beth's mom sat across from Linda, rigid with self-control, and looking as though she might crack into a million pieces if she moved. Only her fingers, spasmodically kneading her wadded handkerchief, betrayed her. *They didn't know if Beth would make it.*

Hospitals were so impersonal. Everything was so routine. The personnel were well-trained robots with mechanical answers. When she'd called from home to find out about Beth, the cool voice of the woman at the switchboard had told her nothing—absolutely nothing.

She'd turned to Dad. "I've got to go," she pleaded. "I have to know. Beth. She—"

"Put on a jacket," Dad said. "I'll drive you. You can't help, but you won't hinder."

The office attendant belonged to the same robot family as the other woman. She passed out pat phrases as though she were handing you a calling card. But she had directed them to this waiting room. Beth's parents had seemed so grateful—that first minute—to see her.

"She's still in emergency." Mrs. Fields clung to her momentarily. "She's still unconscious."

When Dad left, Linda had stayed. She'd thought that perhaps just being with the Fieldses might help. But nothing helped them—or her. Two nurses passed the door. Their cheerful voices charged into the room like blasphemy, and Linda glanced quickly from Mr. to Mrs. Fields. Their expressions didn't change. They hadn't heard. Now Mrs. Fields was murmuring something. Linda bent near to hear.

"She's almost finished her gown," she said. "Just a little sewing left." She looked at Linda and a small smile played across her face. "She was so happy," she said, "so happy you and she were doubling."

Beth, grid queen. Beth— *But we weren't doubling,* Linda said to herself.

"Remember—remember that first game? Remember how Beth cheered?" Mrs. Fields' voice was just above a whisper. Linda nodded. She remembered. And now this.

How had it happened? She didn't know much more than what Tim had told them when he came back from the phone—just that Steve was driving, had taken a corner too fast for the rain-slicked street, and had skidded and crashed into a retaining wall. And that Beth—Beth had been thrown from the car. And, as Vickie said, she'd been hurt badly.

The door opened, and Mr. Fields stopped his pacing momentarily. Reverend Gilmore, their minister. He clasped hands briefly with Mr. Fields, then turned to Mrs. Fields.

"It's so long." Mrs. Fields' voice shook with tears. "It's taking so long. And there's nothing we can do."

"We can pray."

Linda bowed her head and closed her eyes with the

others. But her mind couldn't concentrate on the minister's words. This was their petition, their private petition. She didn't belong.

"The Lord giveth, and taketh away." The words flashed across her mind, and she wanted to erase them. Not Beth. It couldn't mean Beth. She was too young. There were too many things left to do.

The Lord worketh in mysterious ways. Taking Beth would just leave a vacuum. *Please—please—*

A strident, angry, *familiar* voice broke across her plea. The door was flung open, and Mr. Atkins burst into the room. Steve followed. His face was white as he addressed Beth's parents. His eyes looked dazed, unbelieving. "I'm sorry," he said simply. "It's my fault, and I'm sorry."

Linda shuddered at the look of pure hate Mr. Fields turned on him.

"You didn't mean it," said Mrs. Fields. "We know that."

"I've made the necessary arrangements at the office," Mr. Atkins was saying. "I'll handle expenses. She'll get the best of care." His words blared at them as if he were using a loud-speaker. Mr. Fields, fist clenched, face flushed, stepped toward him. Reverend Gilmore laid a restraining hand on his arm. "Why, you—" He looked at his fist, dropped it by his side. "Get out!" he commanded. "Just get out."

Mr. Atkins looked astonished. "You don't understand, Fields," he said. "I'm offering to help."

"Harold, Harold," murmured Mrs. Fields. "He means well. Don't you see?"

Mr. Fields turned aside abruptly.

"Coffee, anyone?" The words came as a shock, and Linda looked up to see a volunteer come into the room with a tray laden with cups and a carafe of coffee, which she put down on the table. "I hadn't expected such a full house," she said. "I'll get more cups."

"I'll help you." Linda sprang to her feet, desperate to escape the hostilities of the room.

"Me too." Steve followed them out the door.

As they kept up with the brisk steps of the volunteer—Linda noticed that her name tag said she was Mrs. Calloway—Linda saw for the first time that Steve was limping rather badly, and she realized, with a twinge of guilt, that not once since she'd heard of the accident had she given a thought to Steve. Mrs. Calloway slowed her pace.

"It's the waiting that's so bad," Steve said.

"The girl in the accident." Mrs. Calloway paused after she seemed to identify them. "My grandmother always said, 'Comparisons are odious,' but—my little girl fell off a horse in a supermarket—one of those mechanical monsters. She was knocked unconscious. She—it was an eternity while we waited. But she was fine." Mrs. Calloway handed Linda the tray with cups and another carafe of coffee. "I think the people in that room need this," she added. The sympathy in her voice made Linda want to cry.

"I keep seeing her. One minute she was laughing, and the next—she lay so still."

Steve's ragged sigh made Linda look at him quickly. Small beads of perspiration glistened on his forehead, and his face had a drawn, white look about it. "Your leg—is it very bad?" she asked. "I didn't even know you'd been hurt."

"My knee, just my knee. I didn't want Beth hurt—ever. I wish it was me, that we could change places. It was my fault." He held the door open and she put the tray down on the table next to the first one. No one had even started to pour.

For a while the silence was broken only by the clink of cup on saucer and her questions "Cream? Sugar?" It was a hate-filled silence, with animosity bristling in almost tangible form from Mr. Fields and Mr. Atkins. Steve— it was as though she were seeing him for the first time. His arrogance, his conceit—had she just *imagined* him as an unfeeling tin god? She had just poured Mrs. Fields a second cup of coffee when the door opened and a doctor gestured to the Fieldses. Mrs. Fields almost knocked the cup of coffee from Linda's hands as she hurried to him, followed by Mr. Fields and Reverend Gilmore. The door closed behind them.

"Ungrateful people." Mr. Atkins dismissed them. "They didn't seem to understand what I was offering." He broke off. "And you!"

For a moment Linda thought Mr. Atkins was addressing her, but his angry gaze was turned on Steve.

"You've jeopardized your whole future, because you were in too much of a hurry to drive some stupid little girl home."

"Dad," Steve warned.

"I spent most of the day for you, so you'd have it made. And you toss it away—your future, *everything*. Do you realize you've probably played your last game of football? How you—"

"You surely can't think he meant to," Linda interrupted.

Mr. Atkins whirled on her. "You shut up!" he commanded. "I'm sick of your do-good meddling. Do you understand?"

Linda shrank against the chair as she had this morning. He turned back to Steve. "Everything—that's what I've done for you. And this is my thanks. A bum knee. And not, excusably, during a football game. Oh no, not that. Over some twit of a girl."

"Dad," Steve warned again, "don't talk like that. Beth's not some girl. She's *my* girl. She—"

Linda saw Steve jerk to his feet, his face chalk-white. Mrs. Fields was at the door, fumbling with the knob, tears streaming down her face. *No, oh no. No, no, no.* Linda stumbled across the room, only she felt as though someone else was doing the moving. Her world was rocking crazily again. She couldn't breathe.

"Linda"—Mrs. Fields crushed Linda to her—"Linda, she's —she's all right. Beth is all right." She held Linda at arm's length. "You may see her—for just a second."

Slowly Linda's world righted itself. Mrs. Fields was crying for joy.

Pale Beth, quiet Beth, sleeping Beth. Her head was swathed in a bandage, her left leg in a bulky cast. As Linda stood close to the bed Beth's eyelids flickered and she murmured something. Linda leaned close to hear.

"Steve. They won't—where's Steve?"

"He's fine."

Beth's hands fluttered on the white spread, restless, helpless. Her eyes flickered open again, and Linda read their plea.

She turned to Mr. Fields. "May Steve come in for just a second?"

"Let him," said Reverend Gilmore.

Mr. Fields nodded.

Linda hurried down the hall. The waiting room was empty. She almost ran to the lobby. Mr. Atkins—she could hear his angry voice. She caught up with them. "Steve —if you want to see Beth for just a minute—"

Steve had started down the hall before she finished her sentence. Linda turned to follow, but Mr. Atkins caught her arm.

"Feeling better?" he asked. "Now that Steve's ruined?" His venomous glare made her want to cringe. He dropped her arm and she hurried up the hall after Steve.

In a matter of minutes Reverend Gilmore was driving her home. Beth's parents wanted to stay at the hospital a little longer, just to reassure themselves. As the car stopped in front of her house Reverend Gilmore laid his hand over Linda's. "Your being there helped them," he said. He glanced at his watch and Linda followed his gaze. "Early enough for me to make another call," he said. "Good night."

"Good night." Linda stood for a minute and watched Reverend Gilmore drive away. She walked to her door. Just two hours, a bare two hours since Tim had first told them, since Vickie had called. It had seemed so—*forever*.

Dad opened the door and she faced her family, waiting, anxious.

"They thought Beth had a fractured skull," she said, "only it wasn't. It's a concussion. And she has a broken leg. The small bone. Tibia, or something like that."

"And Steve?" Tim asked. "No one seems to know about him."

"He and his dad, I saw them both. Steve's limping. He hurt his knee."

"There goes our game." Tim sounded disgusted. "We lose the championship."

"Thank God Beth will be all right," said Mom. She looked at Linda. "You'd better take a hot bath and get into bed. It's still early, I know, but it's been quite a day. I'll bring up a cup of hot chocolate when you're in bed."

"And," added Dad, "you'd better decide to give a little more explanation of your morning drive tomorrow. You and I are to be in your principal's office at eight-fifteen."

A bath and cup of chocolate later, Linda leaned against her pillow. If only she could be thoughtless for just a little while. But the day's events crowded in on her, a hodge-podge of happenings, waiting to make sense. The day was a collage, something like George made up once for the sports page. Had Mr. Benning set her editorial yet? Steve. Everyone cared more about his football than him, it seemed. Did he know? Beth, looking so unnatural in a hospital bed. . . . Doug. Linda looked at her hand as though she hadn't seen it before, and pressed it against her cheek. Doug . . . Mr. Atkins . . . Quite a day, as Dad said. What else could happen in her twenty-four-hour pact?

CHAPTER 21

DAY OF RECKONING

As soon as she awakened in the morning Linda phoned the hospital. All she learned was that Beth spent "a quiet night." Hospitals must have a repertoire of evasive answers. *We're talking about Beth, my best friend,* she'd wanted to protest. Instead she asked that Beth be told she called, and hung up politely. She hugged her robe to her. The morning was chilly. Well, it had a right to be, since Thanksgiving was just a week off. The day was crisp and clear. Yesterday's storm was over.

She took her plaid skirt from its hanger and noticed the blue dress she'd worn that long-ago day when she'd asked Doug to the dance. Doug. In just a few hours he'd be cleared. Because she was going to clear him. She'd made her up her mind for sure. Only first she had to meet with Mr. Marsh with nothing to say. One thing, she'd never bargain time away again. Time was such a funny thing. It was mechanically measured on a clock. It never varied. But for her, time dragged its heels—or swished by.

Breakfast was a hurried affair. It was also rather subdued. Having Dad's presence requested by a principal was never pleasant: heretofore it had happened only with the boys, never with Linda. Tim, Jeff, and Johnny looked their disapproval. Girls were expected to be good.

Dad parked across the street from Claremar's gym. He came around and opened the door for Linda. It was just about *here* that she and Vickie had stood the night Steve and Bob threw water balloons. And *there* where Steve and Doug collided.

"All set, princess?" Dad touched her arm gently. "Remember, I'm with you. All ways."

Mr. Marsh was seated in his office when they were ushered in. He stood, greeted Dad, bade them be seated, and turned to Linda. "Well," he said, "would you care to explain your cut?"

"I—drove around."

"That's all you care to say?"

Linda nodded.

"At least we're sure of one stop you made, Linda." Mr. Marsh handed her a galley proof and gave a second to her father.

Her editorial. The black print screamed her condemning accusations. A few sentences had been deleted, an occasional word changed, but it was the editorial she'd dropped off at Mr. Benning's yesterday morning. Dad's expression was unfathomable as he read. He finished, looked up.

"Quite an article," he said. "Strong words."

"I agree." Mr. Marsh looked at Linda. "Just one thing. I will not tolerate a sneak."

Linda recoiled as if Mr. Marsh had slapped her. She could feel the color rush to her cheeks. She saw Dad half rise in his chair. "Just a minute," he protested. "Hold on a minute."

"Coincidence plays funny tricks," Mr. Marsh continued.

"Mr. Hall seldom calls at the printer's. Yesterday he had a personal errand, and Benning, elated, mentioned the editorial as 'the best [he'd] set in years' and pointed out specific sentences." Mr. Marsh bent his gaze on Linda. "Mr. Hall was surprised. Shocked would be a better word. Here was a substitute editorial sneaked in by a most reliable student. What made you do it, Linda?"

"To make sure it ran." Linda stole a glance at her father. He looked stunned.

"You're suggesting that Mr. Hall or I would have censored it. Right?"

Linda nodded.

"Does Mr. Hall make a practice of censoring your material?"

"No, but this was different. I never wrote an editorial like this before."

"So you presumed to judge Mr. Hall."

"I couldn't take a chance, that's all."

"You talk of fair play, of shouldering responsibilities, and of the evils in 'covering up.' You suggest that the school and community 'cover up' when we ignore facts. You believe this?"

"Yes."

"Your pay-as-you-go plan is unique and cleverly phrased. But just what sin are we as a school not paying for? What, specifically, are you referring to?"

Linda kept her gaze on the books in her lap.

"Come now, Linda." Mr. Marsh's voice showed his irritation. "Let's have some facts. What are you referring to?"

Linda glanced desperately at the clock. How could her twenty-four-hour truce with Mr. Atkins last so long?

"Tell him, Linda," Dad said softly. "Tell him about the accident."

Linda wet her lips and swallowed.

"The accident had nothing to do with this editorial, Mr. Chapin." Mr. Marsh flicked the galley proof with his finger. "This was turned in some time yesterday morning before the accident occurred."

"The collision a few weeks ago involving Steve Atkins and Doug Johnson," Dad elaborated.

"Your editorial refers to that?"

Linda nodded.

"Hmm." Mr. Marsh laid the proof down and picked up the copy she'd turned in. "Taken in that light . . . you feel the police are remiss too? None of us is spared." He pursed his lips and studied Linda. "I'm beginning to see motive," he said. "And perhaps, in a matter of minutes . . ." He glanced at the clock, then returned his gaze to Linda. "But first we have some unpleasant business. You are aware of the consequences of a cut?"

"Failing grades for a day."

"That's a start. And the editorial?"

Linda's throat felt parched, her lips dry. Suspension? Expulsion?

"I asked you to be present, Mr. Chapin, because of what I have to do. Penalties for first cuts are often mild. But the flagrant disregard for rules—this editorial—" He hesitated. "First I should tell you, Linda, that the editorial is running with only your libelous phrases removed. Because it is good writing with an excellent message."

"Thank you."

"Ordinarily you'd be dropped from the *Clarion* staff automatically. You know that. Perhaps you should be. But with your writing talent we feel that if you give us your word, if you'll promise—"

"I do. Oh, I do," interrupted Linda.

"Your advisor and I thought you would." Linda felt relief engulf her. "However," Mr. Marsh continued, "on one matter we have no choice. I'm writing a letter today to have your name taken off the exchange list."

Linda felt wooden, unable to move. Thinking of consequences, even expecting them, wasn't like getting them.

"You never explained, Linda," Dad protested. "Tell Mr. Marsh the circumstances—or I will."

"No circumstances change facts, Mr. Chapin." Mr. Marsh leaned across his desk. "The citizenship record of an exchange student has to be above reproach. Linda has discredited herself on two counts. The list of applicants is long, the competition keen. Any disqualification that narrows the field . . . I'm sorry."

"I understand," Dad said heavily.

Linda didn't want to understand. She wanted to flip back time. *Pay as you go,* she'd written. It was ironic she should be the first. Mr. Marsh talked briefly on his phone and stood up. "I hadn't planned to include you in this next meeting, but I think it important that you stay."

The door opened and she saw Doug, Bob, Steve, Mr. Atkins, and the police chief enter. "Linda Chapin, who's on our *Clarion* staff, her father, Mr. Chapin," said Mr. Marsh, beginning introductions.

After his first look of surprise at seeing Linda and her dad, Mr. Atkins' expression changed to stony scorn as he leveled his gaze on her. She wanted to squirm out of its reach, and stole a glance at the boys. Steve's face was unreadable; Bob showed neither surprise nor recognition. Doug's half smile as he caught her eye seemed to reflect troubled concern for her, or was she reading into expressions what she wanted to see?

"We'll get to facts," Mr. Marsh stated as he concluded the introductions.

"It's pretty much the way we figured," said the chief. "Johnson's in the clear about the beer." He turned to Doug. "You can thank your boss for insisting you weren't the drinking kind."

"He's been great," agreed Doug.

"The beer?" asked Mr. Marsh.

"Since it was an import and not too popular around here it was easy to track down. Only one store carries it—as a favor to Mr. Atkins. No other purchasers."

"It's revenge," broke in Mr. Atkins. "The whole lot of you want revenge. When my boy was okay you let him play. You keep your eyes shut when it's convenient, don't you? But the minute he's laid up—"

"So you admit the beer was yours?" Mr. Marsh looked as if he were having difficulty keeping his temper.

"Admit? What else when this snip of a girl's been blabbing?" Mr. Atkins turned on Linda. "A fine one to talk of honor when you couldn't keep a bargain for twenty-four hours. Yesterday, in the office, you and I—"

"Linda," interrupted her father, "did you go to see Mr. Atkins?"

Linda nodded.

"You didn't know?" Mr. Atkins turned his stunned gaze on Linda's dad. "That's not why we're here?"

"My time's not up yet," Linda said simply.

"Perhaps," said Mr. Marsh, "we should stop this confusion and get to fundamentals. What information are you withholding, Linda."

She drew a shaky breath. She didn't dare look over at Steve, at Doug, at Bob. "It was about the beer," she said.

"It concerns me, sir." Bob stepped forward. "She heard me put the beer in Johnson's car. Might as well admit it. You must know, anyway."

"Right," said the chief. "When we started investigating, one of the officers recalled seeing Steve take you aside. It was a few minutes before you joined the others."

"Was this what you were going to say?" Mr. Marsh addressed Linda.

"Just about." She turned to the chief. "I owe you an apology for doubting."

"We're used to it. Too many people have the wrong image of the police, a blanket belief that cops are fixed, politicians are crooked, newspapermen are drunks, jurors can be bought, kids are delinquent." The chief paused for breath. "The occasional bad one is publicized; the rest of us get his brand." He looked at Mr. Marsh. "Sorry to have taken the floor," he said, "but it gets me, the public's attitude toward police. My men are honest and hard-working."

"We appreciate that," said Mr. Marsh.

"Now, if you'll excuse me," the chief continued, "we seem to have wound up everything that concerns my department here. . . . I've an appointment."

As the chief left, Mr. Marsh wrote on his memo pad, then tore off the page. "Your admit to class, Doug," he said. "No reason to keep you here any longer." He handed Doug the paper. "I suppose you were among the doubters?"

Doug gave an embarrassed laugh. "I guess so, sir. I didn't think I had a chance. I figured I was pretty lucky my dad was with me all the way, and my boss—he's a great guy, and . . ."

"I can see you had more cause than, say, Linda, to doubt," interrupted Mr. Marsh. "But if you young people would just be a little slower jumping to conclusions . . ."

Linda didn't look up until Doug had closed the door behind him.

Mr. Marsh turned his attention to Bob. "No point in a lecture now," he said. "You're well aware of the consequences, I'm sure." He handed Bob his admit. "Suspension from all sports for the remainder of the year, and of course you aren't eligible for any athletic awards. Any questions?"

"No, sir." Bob's hand shook as he took the admit. He looked grim.

Now there were just the four of them—five, including Mr. Marsh. "Steve, Linda, I may as well write admits for you also." Mr. Marsh paused in his writing. "Any comment from either of you?"

Linda looked at Steve. At this point she felt fortunate not to get academic suspension as well as her other penalty. Maybe Steve felt the same way.

Mr. Atkins broke the silence. "I have something to say. We can still salvage the most important thing, Steve's All-Star award. He can't play this last game, granted. But his knee can be the obvious, publicized reason." His voice picked up enthusiasm. "He can still be—"

Mr. Marsh shook his head impatiently. "You don't understand, Mr. Atkins," he said. "Steve's through with sports this year."

"Agreed. And that should please the two of you." Mr. Atkins' gesture included Linda. "But, as I say, he can still make All-Star. I spent most of yesterday making contacts, calling the right people. And from the inferences, Steve's the choice. He fills the qualifications—good job on the field, played a winning game, showed—"

"He's disqualified himself on several counts, Mr. Atkins." Mr. Marsh stood tall. "He has been suspended from sports."

"Only if you're too petty to let things ride. Only if you talk." Mr. Atkins pounded his fist in his hand to emphasize the words. "Listen to reason, man. This may be Steve's last chance—*his last chance*. Because of his knee he may never play football again. He deserves recognition. He's earned it. And—I—if you just let things ride—I can pick up the tabs. That boy's—the chief's—"

"Your inference is insulting." Mr. Marsh looked furious. "You can't buy justice."

"It's been done."

"Dad, please." Steve had stood up and put his hand on his father's arm as if he were trying to restrain him. "Don't say any more. I'm sorry I did this to you. If I could undo it—but I can't. It's true, what they say. I'm through. I'm kaput. There's no way out."

"But there is. The right contacts, the right strings—"

"No, Dad. No. I had this coming. Last night, waiting at the hospital, I had plenty of time to think. It was—ah—it was rough." Steve struggled to control his emotion. "Because it's my fault, and only mine, that Beth's in the hospital now. And maybe, if I'd faced up before, Beth wouldn't be there."

"You're telling me hands off, keep out, you don't need me any more." Mr. Atkins spoke in a monotone.

"Don't need you? Dad, this— I had it coming, but it still hurts. I'm going to need you and Mom more than ever."

Mr. Marsh cleared his throat. "I think we'd better terminate this gathering," he said brusquely. "As a group we're getting nowhere. Linda, Steve, your admits." He handed them the papers. "So, if you'll excuse me . . ."

The suddenness of their dismissal was a shock. Linda followed her father out of the office. Steve and his dad— she watched them walk down the hall. Could people change stature before your eyes? Somehow, it seemed that Steve was the stronger of the two.

"I'm sorry, princess, the way things worked out for you," Dad said.

"I made you lose the contract."

"No, Linda, you didn't. I phoned Mr. Atkins yesterday morning and suggested that, under the circumstances, he contact another builder. It was the only thing I could do if even a little of what you were suggesting was true. So you see, I lost it on my own."

She'd been in the office when he'd phoned. That's why Mr. Atkins had bargained for time, why he'd made the contacts he'd mentioned. Because Dad was no longer a bargaining point. Dad—how could she have doubted him? Tears sprung to her eyes.

"Chin up, sweets." Dad brushed her chin lightly with his fist. "See you at supper." He turned and strode quickly down the hall.

Linda felt deserted even as she realized that Dad was helping her. He knew sympathy made her weepy, so he'd walked away. The hall was empty before her. She clutched her books for support as she started down the corridor. Her footsteps made a rhythm for the phrase that kept repeating itself. *Lost the chance to go to France.* She pushed open her classroom door.

By noon Claremar High *knew.* And what wasn't known was rumored. Doug Johnson became hero to some, villain to others. Steve was thought abused, misused, or a dirty rat. Most everyone seemed sorry about Beth.

The cafeteria looked chaotic. Linda decided to buy an apple at the vending machine and walk with Vickie and Mary Lou as they ate their sandwiches.

"Beth will have to drop Steve," Vickie announced. "He's through."

"And how!" agreed Mary Lou.

Linda was about to say that she didn't think Beth had any intention of dropping Steve when a group of girls enveloped them.

"Say, Vickie, didn't you and Linda see the accident?" a girl asked. "Aren't they calling you as witnesses or something?"

"Because Steve and Bob were drunk, that's why," said a second girl.

"They're always drunk, everybody knows that," another added.

Linda looked at the speaker in disgust, then glanced at Vickie.

"Linda and I only heard the accident," Vickie corrected.

She looked both amused and flattered by the attention she was getting.

"I bet Steve was drunk yesterday," said the first girl. "I mean, after all . . ."

"Oh." Mary Lou gave a little shiver. "It's all too absolutely *grue*."

Linda turned away, feeling ill. *Absolutely gruesome* was a gruesomely apt description of these gossip-hungry girls. And it wasn't that they meant to be malicious, it was just that they didn't hesitate to mutilate facts if it made a more dramatic story. Somehow they were forgetting that Steve and Bob and Beth and Doug were *people*.

CHAPTER 22

FINAL SCORE

Dad's white shirt crinkled in starched protest under Linda's heavy sweater as she shifted position. This section of the bleachers must look dazzling with all its white-shirted rooters. She looked at Doug wedged beside her. He met her glance with a wink and a smile and took a firmer grasp of her hand as he turned his attention back to the football field. The score was Hillhaven 7, Claremar 0, and it was half time at the Thanksgiving Day Big-Little game.

A week ago Linda had wondered if this day would ever arrive. And then she'd been afraid of what it would be like when it did. Judging from the way the townspeople were jammed into the bleachers, Steve's and Bob's suspension from the team had merely whetted their football appetite.

The lead held by Hillhaven had been hard won. As Coach Wallace predicted yesterday, Claremar's eleven were fighting to win—every minute of play. "A team isn't made up of a couple of players," he'd said.

George, already hoarse from the first half, was giving a rundown of half-time events. She wondered what he'd say Monday when he heard her exciting news. "You've committed verbal hari-kari," he'd commented after reading her editorial.

Hillhaven's band had completed their field formation. As

Claremar's band precision-marched for grandstand approval the cheerleaders gestured wildly for applause. A fresh wave of cheers ran through the bleachers as Claremar's grid queen and her attendants drove slowly by. Linda swallowed the lump in her throat. Just a minute's carelessness had eliminated Beth from the race. Now she sat in the bottom row, a Claremar's colors toe-sock decorating her cumbersome cast. Steve sat beside her, holding her crutches. Bob was at the game too. He and Steve—it took guts for them to come. Every minute of play must be a bitter reminder. But they were taking it—not like Steve's parents, who had flown to Hawaii for a few days.

Linda went through the card stunts automatically. Mom, Dad, the twins, her grandparents—could they see the card mosaics? Or were Hillhaven rooters the main recipients? Dad really was going to be pleased with her news. "That's my princess," he'd say.

Now Claremar's rooting section tore the cards into bits and tossed the colored scraps into the air. "Here they come, princess." Doug reached for her hand as Linda saw the teams run onto the field while bands and baton twirlers swirled off. They raced through their program of calisthenics; then the two elevens were facing each other in formation, Claremar receiving the kickoff to the roll of drums. They returned the ball, ten, fifteen, eighteen yards. First down.

"We want a touchdown!" chanted Claremar rooters. *Win, win, win,* added Linda inwardly.

By the fourth quarter the score was still Hillhaven 7, Claremar 0. Both teams battled every foot of the way. The teams changed goals, and it was Claremar's ball. They marched yard by yard, play by play, to Hillhaven's twenty-two-yard line, then lost it on downs. Hillhaven made first down on the next play, then—then somebody fumbled, and it was Claremar's ball again. The physical strain of the players on the field seemed to extend right into the rooting section as Claremar pushed for a measured first down. Now the rooters were going crazy. *"Go, go, go!"* The chant throbbed through the bleachers. *"Go, go, go!"*

A fumble. Claremar's. A distressed moan spilled from the rooters and echoed the length of the bleachers. A unified sigh rippled in its wake as they discovered that Claremar had recovered.

Another painful, battering first down and Claremar was on the four-yard line, goal to go. Now time was against them. Steve, Bob, how they were needed now!

"Go, go, go!" *"We want a touchdown!"* *"Hold that line!"* *"Hey, hey, take it away!"* Chants rose from the cheering sections like war cries, tearing the air to shreds. *". . . team isn't made up of a couple of players . . . we'll have eleven fighters. . . ."* But oh, how those couple of players could help! Three minutes. Third down.

"A fake around left end." Doug breathed the words. *"He made it."*

Pandemonium broke out in Claremar's rooting section. Then dead silence. The kick. *How could one guy endure the strain?* Linda almost didn't want to watch. *It was too much for one person.* The cheerleaders had raced to the goal posts. The air was utterly still, broken only by the referee's whistle. Toe against leather. You could hear the boot. The ball wavered, then sailed between the goal posts. Hillhaven 7, Claremar 7. George's voice cracked as he gave

189

the score. For all practical purposes, the game was over. Linda flexed crushed fingers as Doug released her hand.

The final gun went off. The bleachers emptied slowly. Doug guided her through the crowd, hands on her waist. She heard Mary Lou scream, "Isn't it perf?" and turned and waved. She saw Tim, hands clasped high in victory. But it hadn't been victory, really. It simply hadn't been defeat. Once outside the gate, the crowd thinned.

"Mind walking, princess?" Doug asked.

"I love walking." Linda anchored her hand in Doug's firm clasp. Soon she'd tell him her good news. Right now it was enough to walk along without speaking, absorbing, sort of, the *goodness* of Thanksgiving.

All over town families would be gathering soon to crack worn jokes and pass the turkey platter. Steve would be at Beth's. And, her parents willing, Linda would join them this evening for checkers or Old Maid. Since the second accident, she and Beth had been closer than ever. She wished Doug were able to go with her, but, well, when Mom and Dad had invited him and his mother for Thanksgiving, he'd proudly declined. His dad and sister were flying in. They had reservations for a real family re-union.

A car of cheering Claremar rooters roared past. "They can thank Hillhaven's fumble," Doug commented. "That was our break."

A good break for Claremar, a bad one for Hillhaven—just that one fumble. Life was like that. You fumbled, lost—or recovered. Like she'd lost the scholarship. Only she'd recovered too, because just before she left home for the game the call had come—from the *Herald* editor, saying he wanted permission to reprint her editorial, and would she like to be Claremar High's correspondent for the *Herald*—a job created especially for her. If only she could have shared her excitement! But she'd been the only one home. Now she would wait until dinner. She could just *see* Dad's reaction . . .

Doug squeezed her hand hard. "Come back, Linda," he commanded. "You've been a long way off." He smiled at her and the crinkles around his eyes showed. "Hi, princess, honey," he said.

His words enveloped her. They made her feel as if she were on the verge of a brand-new exciting beginning of something. They made her want to share her news with him *right now*.

"Hi, Doug—honey," she said. "Guess what?"

ABOUT THE AUTHOR

ANNE ALEXANDER lives in Burlingame, California, and is the mother of three daughters, two of whom are married and have children of their own. Her house is continually overflowing with her young grandchildren and her youngest daughter's college friends. These different visitors have supplied the author with material for many magazine articles, picture books for very young children, and teen-age novels.

Mrs. Alexander was born in Shanghai, China, where her mother was a missionary nurse and her father the captain of a British river boat. She came to this country when she was twelve years old and later married Charles Alexander, a newspaperman. Mrs. Alexander recently received an Associated Arts degree from College of San Mateo.

H52

F
ALE
ALEXANDER, ANNE
Linda

6 4 90

DATE DUE			
MAY 9 '72	DEC 20 '73	JAN 24 '78	
MAY 4 '72	JAN 21 '74		
OCT 11 '72	FEB 7 '74		
NOV 7 '72	FEB 19 '75		
DEC 14 '72	NOV 22 '75		
APR 11 '73	DEC 16 1976		
SEP 18 '73	OCT 11 '77		
OCT 12 '73	NOV 15 '77		
OCT 24 '73	JAN 3 '78		
NOV. 7 '73	JAN 20 '78		
DEC 17 '73	SEP '74		ALESCO